Other books by Dr. Mary Ellen Erickson

Grandma Mary & Bonbon series: *First Day of School, Snowstorm, and Bonbon's Special Christmas*. Children's picture books that teach character-building traits and emphasize rules and work ethics.

Peanut Butter Club Mystery series: *What Happened to the Deer?, Who Jinxed the C&G Ranch?, and Did Bigfoot Steal Christmas?*. This series is full of fun and adventure and emphasizes responsibility, friendship, and the special relationship between grandparents and grandchildren.

Common Sense Caregiving: A nonfiction adult book based on research that stresses the positive side of caring for the elderly.

Humble and Homemade: Survival in Tough Times: An adult nonfiction book of short stories, cooking and gardening that shows you how to make the very best of what you already have.

Otis: An historical-fiction novel that includes humor, romance, mystery and some complicated family relationships.

Geezettes: Books 1 and 2: Adult novels about retired women. This series emphasizes humor, romance, and the importance of friendships as we grow older.

Visit Dr. Mary's Website for more information:
www.drmarysbooks.com

Dontcha Know?

A Cozy Mystery with Humor

Mary Ellen Erickson, PhD

DONTCHA KNOW?
A COZY MYSTERY WITH HUMOR

iUniverse books may be ordered through booksellers or by contacting:

iUniverse
1663 Liberty Drive
Bloomington, IN 47403
www.iuniverse.com
1-800-Authors (1-800-288-4677)

ISBN: 978-1-4917-9318-3 (sc)
ISBN: 978-1-4917-9317-6 (e)

Library of Congress Control Number: 2016905708

Print information available on the last page.

iUniverse rev. date: 04/21/2016

CHAPTER 1

Toto, I've a feeling we're not in Kansas anymore.
—*The Wizard of Oz* (1939)

She was called Gen by her friends, but her full name was Genevieve Grace Gorman Fletcher. She was young and inexperienced, but nobody was going to tell her where she could go and what she should do.

Spring had come late this year, so the trees weren't fully budded out. The variety of evergreens in the thickly wooded areas along the roadside made the scenery—what you could see of it— green. The farther north she drove, the more wintery the roadsides looked. Occasionally she spied a small patch of snow nestled at the foot of a shaded patch of evergreens. It was the first week of April 2013, and northern Minnesota was still feeling the pains of winter. The paved road seemed to grow narrower the farther north she went.

The last sign of life she'd seen was two hours ago when she'd stopped at a gas station on the north side of Bemidji to fill the Ford Fusion for the last 120 miles of her trip.

"You'll be living in the wilds with moose, deer, and bears!" Fletch had scoffed when she'd announced her decision.

Evan Patrick Fletcher had been against this move from the minute she'd gotten the phone call asking her to finish the school year for a missing high school teacher who'd been teaching in Little Beaver, Minnesota.

"I'm sick and tired of substitute teaching in St. Cloud. I hate these big towns and big schools," Gen had retaliated. She had been born and raised in a small southwestern Minnesota farming community; small towns were her forte.

Gen and Fletch had met at Moorhead State University when she was enrolled in a secondary-education course with majors in history and English. Fletch was a business major with minors in banking and finance. His great physique, handsome features, intelligence, and soft-spoken, friendly nature had attracted Gen from the start. They'd fallen in love and gotten married the summer after they both graduated. Fletch had gotten a job as a loan officer in a large Wells Fargo bank in St. Cloud, so they moved to that bustling city after their marriage, got a nice apartment, and set up housekeeping.

Gen hadn't been lucky enough to find a teaching job in St. Cloud, so she'd been substituting in the St. Cloud school system for almost two years and was sick of it. She felt she needed a chance to be in her own classroom, doing her own thing. She had accumulated so many ideas on how she was going to teach during her own secondary-school years and the four years she spent at Moorhead State; now she wanted to try some of them. Gen knew that if she were given the chance, she could be the world's best teacher—but then, didn't all starting teachers feel that way?

"Ahhhhhhhh!" Gen screamed as she slammed on the brakes to miss a young doe that had suddenly sprung out of the ditch on the left side of the road.

Gen's head glanced against the steering wheel when the car slammed to a stop in the ditch on the right side of the road. "Ohhh," she moaned, rubbing her head while trying to remember what had happened.

"Dang deer," she muttered. *I hope I didn't hit it. If I wreck the car, Fletch will smirk all the more.* She could see his face now, smiling his know-it-all smile. *"Told you so,"* he'd say.

Gen slowly opened the car door and got out to assess the damage. There was no deer lying in the ditch. *Thank God,* she thought with a sigh.

The car seemed to be okay except for the front and back wheels on the right side of the car, which were embedded in some soft dirt on the shoulder of the road. The left wheels, thankfully, were still on the road.

How will I get out of this mess? she thought. *I'll probably be here for days before someone comes along to help me.* "No," she said out loud, while clearing her mind. *This is a paved road, and they wouldn't pave a road nobody used. There have to be people who drive on this road.*

Gen opened the back door and got back into the car to check the things in the back seat that had fallen on the floor when the car had come to an abrupt halt. She was lucky nothing had hit her on the head and knocked her out. She was straightening up the mess when she heard the roar of a pickup motor; it sounded like someone's muffler was missing.

Gen got out of the car and saw the ten-plus-year-old red GMC pickup speeding down the road. As the pickup approached, it didn't seem to make any effort to slow down, so she jumped back into the car because she was afraid she might get run over.

The person in the pickup saw the damsel in distress and slammed on his brakes as he passed her car. It took almost a hundred feet and a lot of rubber on the pavement before the pickup stopped. In a cloud of smoke, the man backed up and got out of his truck. Tall, dark, and handsome with a full beard, the thirty-something male was wearing a tight pair of blue jeans and a red plaid shirt. He looked like the statue of Paul Bunyan she'd seen in Bemidji two hours ago.

"Howdy. Got a problem?" he asked in a patronizing way, standing tall with his hands in his pockets.

"Ya think?" Gen looked amused. *What a male chauvinist,* she thought.

"Need help?"

"Yeah, thanks."

"I'll have you out in a jiff. I always carry a tow rope."

Gen watched Paul Bunyan saunter over to the back of his pickup, pull out a heavy rope from the truck box, and hook it onto the back of her Ford; then he walked back to his pickup.

Man, he's got a good-looking set of tight buns, she thought.

"Get into your car, start it, and put it in reverse," he ordered, looking at her with dark, piercing eyes. "When you feel a jerk, step on the gas and try to back up as I pull."

He jumped into his pickup after she got her car started. He started the truck and slowly drove forward until the rope became taut. As the rope jerked the car, Gen stepped on the gas, and slowly the car rolled back up out of the ditch and onto the road.

When she was back on the road, Gen stopped the car and got out to look for any damage that might have been done to the wheels or the frame. After assuring herself that all was well, she turned to thank her knight in shining armor, but he was already in his pickup and heading down the road.

Just as well, she thought. *He made me feel like I was a nuisance he had to take care of to retain his manhood.*

Gen ran her fingers through her collar-length, dusky blonde hair. She pushed her half bang, which needed trimming, out of her Mediterranean-blue eyes and put her Serengeti sunglasses back on. She was ready to continue her adventure.

After checking her map, she decided she was at least ten miles from her destination. She drove more cautiously now. The paved road that was full of potholes now turned into a gravel road full of potholes and roots. The roadside was lined with spindly pine trees that were trying to grow in the ditches and hadn't been removed. It was very quiet along this last stretch of empty gravel road that burrowed through the pines.

Almost like magic, there was a clearing in the trees, and a little village, nestled on the shore of a small lake, came into view. The lake was surrounded with balsam fir, white spruce, birch, and jack pine. The edges of the lake had thick growths of rushes and tall grass. Some rushes and foxtail also grew in spots throughout the lake.

She scrutinized the landscape. Rugged beauty greeted her from every angle. "Wow!" Gen mused. "It's beautiful." The awesome landscape stretched out as far as the eye could see.

She drove slowly, winding her way down a sloping hill to the village center. *Now where could the Bumblebee Inn be located?* she asked herself. Then she smiled. *Even if I have to look through the whole town, it won't take too long to find it.*

CHAPTER 2

Wait a minute, wait a minute. You ain't heard nothin' yet!
—*The Jazz Singer* (1927)

As Gen drove down Main Street in Little Beaver, she suddenly realized she was longing for a cup of coffee. Except for her stop for gas near Bemidji about an hour and a half ago, she had driven for about five and a half hours. By this time on a normal day, she would already have had at least two cups of coffee. Drinking coffee during breaks was a habit she had picked up during her years of substitute teaching. The big thirty-cup coffeepot in the teachers' lounge was plugged in all day, and during breaks teachers sat in the lounge and drank coffee, which was a necessary survival tool in the profession.

Gen spotted a sign hanging above the front door of a tall, dilapidated, two-story building: Coffee and Beer. *Probably the two favorite beverages in Little Beaver.* She parked her car directly in front of the building, got out, locked the doors, and entered the front door of the café/bar.

The place was deserted. *It's Saturday*, she thought. *The place should be open.*

Gen called, "Anybody here?"

No answer.

"Yoo-hoo, anybody here?"

Silence.

"Well," she muttered out loud, "maybe you just help yourself."

She looked around. The room she was standing in had a few small tables with chairs around them. *This must be the café*, she thought. To her left was a swinging door that entered into a small, lighted room. *That must be the kitchen.* Straight ahead of her was a double swinging door that went into a large, dark room. *That must be the bar.* There was a soda machine to the left of the tables. *I guess you do help yourself.*

Gen went through the swinging doors on her left and called, "Anyone here?"

No answer.

She went back into the café and sat down at one of the tables to think about what she should do, as she didn't like soda. She pondered her situation.

Seconds later the front door opened and a young woman, dressed in jeans, running shoes, and a T-shirt entered. She was about Gen's age; had long, black, braided, shiny hair; and was tall and thin. Very attractive in an "all-American girl" kind of way.

"Hi," Gen said.

"Hi, yourself," the young women answered with a surprised look on her face. "What are you doing here?"

"This is a café, isn't it?" Gen asked.

"Yeah, sure, you betcha, but we don't see too many strangers in this town. You kinda startled me."

Gen smiled. "I'm looking for a cup of coffee."

"Ed should be here someplace. He's the cook and manages the place. I'll go see if I can find him."

With that said, the young woman went into the kitchen and yelled, "Ed, where the heck are you?"

Soon she emerged with an overweight, middle-aged, slightly balding man who must have been Ed.

"Hi," he said, "I'm Ed. What can I do for you?"

"You got a cup of coffee?" Gen asked.

"Sure, I was just making some."

Where, Gen thought, *in the next county?*

"By the way, I'm Elizabeth Larson; everyone calls me Liz. I run the convenience store down the block."

Liz stuck out her right hand, and Gen shook it. "Glad to meet you, Liz. I'm Gen Fletcher. I'm going to finish the teaching term of the high school teacher who disappeared about ten days ago."

"Is that right?" Liz had a skeptical look on her face as she sat down at the table where Gen was seated.

"Anyone know what happened?" Gen asked.

Liz got up, wandered over to the soda machine, got a Diet Coke, and sat down again. The look on her face seemed to say, *Should I tell her what I know or not?* It looked like she might be trying to protect someone.

"The Koochiching County sheriff did some investigating, but I'm not sure what he found. He seems to be keeping a closed mouth on the subject. I guess they are thinking that Evie just up and left—kids got to her. Pretty rough kids at the high school, dontcha know?"

No, I don't know, Gen thought. Since she had known Evelyn Pretsler back in college, Gen could see her up and leaving without any notice to anyone. Evelyn, "Evie," was an airhead in college and probably hadn't changed in the past year. How Evie had ever gotten a job was a mystery to Gen. But then, not everyone wanted to teach in the coldest spot in the continental United States, where running water was a luxury.

"Well, I've got to get going," Liz stood up and announced with a nervous giggle. "You never know when someone will need a loaf of bread."

"Sure, see you around."

Liz disappeared through the front door, and Gen sat in silence by herself, sipping her coffee. She reminisced about the few times she had been with Evie at college. Evie wasn't bad looking, about five-seven, thin blonde hair, and a nose that was slightly too big for her face.

Gen remembered the times Evie had sneaked out of the dorm around ten at night and returned after midnight. Where she went, nobody knew, but it was rumored she had her pajamas on under her long trench coat. She usually came back into the dorm via the fire-escape window that was left partly open. The dorm door closed at midnight.

The thing about Evie that intrigued Gen the most was the dullness in her eyes. Those eyes always looked like she was bored—no sparkle at all. Evie seemed to be totally indifferent to what was going on around her, a total airhead.

The door flew open, and two elderly gentlemen walked into the restaurant, having a spirited conversation.

"No, that isn't the way it was," the short, white-haired, feisty-looking one said. "I remember 2000 very clearly, and we did *not* win the regional basketball tournament that year!"

"Well, you know," the taller, lanky man mumbled while stroking his chin, "it was one of those years that D.J. played along with all those Indian guys—they were good, darn good!"

The conversation stopped abruptly as the two elderly gentlemen noticed Gen. They looked as though they'd seen a ghost.

"Hello," the short guy said.

The tall guy grunted something and nodded a greeting.

"Hi," Gen replied.

The two walked through the double swinging door that led into the bar and turned on the lights; then they sat down. It was coffee time for a group of senior citizens who met every afternoon, six days a week, at the café/bar for refreshments and stimulating arguments about old times.

In the next ten minutes, four additional older men entered the café and stared at Gen. One greeted her, and two just walked past her like she wasn't there. The last gentleman to enter was a very overweight, big man who walked slowly, trying to move his bulky body along. His salt-and-pepper hair was tied in a ponytail at the nape of his neck. Sparkling black eyes conveyed a sense of humor and intelligence.

He saw Gen, stopped, and smiled. "Well, hello. Who have we here?"

"Hi." Gen smiled back. "I'm Gen Fletcher. I'm the new teacher who will replace Evelyn Pretsler at the high school."

"Okay, glad to meet you. I'm on the school board, so I knew you were coming. Welcome to Little Beaver. Glad you made it okay."

"So am I," Gen replied with a laugh. "The roads aren't the best around here."

"I'm Herman Jacobear. Most call me 'Bear.' I'm part Chippewa, part Norwegian, and part French Canadian—lots of us around here are. Living so close to the Red Lake Indian Reservation, dontcha know."

Gen stuck out her hand. "Glad to meet you, Herman. I guess I did talk to you on the phone. Your name sounds familiar."

"Yes, yes, come join us. I'll introduce you to some of the boys."

Gen picked up her cup of coffee and followed Herman into the inner sanctuary, where the other five men were seated and loudly discussing local affairs.

"Listen up, you old goats!" Herman shouted. The group got quiet. "This here is Gen Fletcher. She's our new teacher. I asked her to come and sit with us so I could look at something pretty for a change, instead of your old, grizzled faces."

All the guys laughed, and one got up and put another chair at the table for Gen to sit on.

Gen sat down and waited. The older gentlemen were a bit smitten by the attractive young woman and stared at her for a moment before warming up to her. Gen's luminous blue eyes, high cheekbones, and straight nose reflected her natural beauty. Her friendly smile was inviting and made them feel comfortable.

Herman introduced his compatriots.

"This is Jack Beane," he said, pointing to the short, feisty man. "He's a retired logger."

"Hi." Jack waved.

"This is Jim Stern," he said of the lanky, slow guy, "who's been retired all his life."

Everyone laughed, and Jim nodded.

"This is Elroy Hoffer, the local banker. Watch out for him."

Elroy was dressed in a business suit. He was of medium height and weight, with a reserved, aristocratic air about him. He looked to be a bit younger than the rest. He nodded and smiled.

"This is Doc Johnson. My advice is don't get sick while you're in Little Beaver. This old curmudgeon will kill you!"

With a deadpan look on his face, Doc joked, "Don't listen to Bear. He's just mad cause I told him if he doesn't lose some weight, he'll die!"

Nobody laughed.

Doc had a surly look about him and seemed a bit grumpy. He projected authority when he spoke.

"Last but not least, this is Foster Graywolfe; he's Ojibwa. He went out into the world, made a million playing professional football, and then came back here to hunt, fish, and die. We all call him 'Wolf.'"

Graywolfe looked at Herman with absolutely no expression on his face and nodded. He was a big man who looked like a former football player. His dark eyes and long, graying ponytail reflected his Native American heritage.

Total silence descended for a moment, as everyone was wondering what to say next. Then Elroy asked a question. "So where are you staying, Gen?"

"At the Bumblebee Inn."

"That's a nice place," Elroy said. "Mrs. Jacobs will take good care of you."

Everyone nodded, and several of the men added comments on the amenities at the inn.

"I understand that Evelyn Pretsler, the last teacher, stayed there too," Gen said.

Again everyone nodded.

"I wonder what happened to her?" Gen asked.

Silence.

"I hope you'll like it here, Mrs. Fletcher." Herman changed the subject.

Everyone now eagerly joined the conversation and took turns asking Gen questions.

"Is Gen your real name?" Jack asked.

"No, it's Genevieve. I hate that name; too many Es." Gen laughed. Nobody laughed with her. *Maybe they didn't know how to spell Genevieve.*

"Where is your husband?" Jim asked.

"Back in St. Cloud, working—I hope!"

Everyone laughed loudly. The men liked that answer.

"What do you teach?" The banker tried to ask an intelligent question.

"History and English."

"That Ford Fusion out front yours?" Doc inquired.

"Yes."

"Humph," Doc mumbled and then spit out a wad of chewing tobacco into his saucer.

Graywolfe didn't ask any questions.

Next each man felt it his duty to advise Gen on some important issue concerning her stay in Little Beaver.

"You'll probably have to eat at the school and Mrs. Jacobs's place. The only other place to eat is here, and all Ed can cook is hamburgers, hot dogs, and pizzas."

Gen laughed along with everyone else. She had already noticed Ed's lack of ambition.

"The only place to fill gas is at the convenience store. Liz runs that. She's a nice lady, dontcha know," Jack enthusiastically offered.

"Thanks, I've already met Liz."

"If you need to do any banking, come in and I'll personally take care of you," Elroy offered.

"Watch out for him," Herman reminded Gen.

Everyone laughed.

"Thanks," Gen said, smiling diffidently at Elroy.

"You'll have to come down here on Tuesday or Friday nights and play Texas hold 'em poker with us," Doc suggested. "It's always nice to have a new pigeon in the flock."

Gen wondered what Doc meant by "pigeon."

Graywolfe did not give any advice.

One hour later Gen knew where everything in town was located, what everyone did, and who to watch out for. She even got to hear a few good jokes that had been cleaned up a bit because a lady was present.

When the jokes and local stories stopped and there was a break in the conversation, Gen stood up. "I'd better go find the Bumblebee Inn and get settled before nightfall—dontcha know?" she said. *Good God*, she thought, *I'm starting to talk like they do.*

"Just follow Main Street north, and you'll see the three-story brick building—that's the school. The Bumblebee Inn is right across the street; you can't miss it," Herman instructed.

"Thanks for all the advice, gentlemen." Gen smiled and headed for the swinging doors.

The guys called out various good wishes as she exited: "Good luck; see you around; come join us again; nice meeting you."

What a great bunch of gentlemen, she thought. *They made my day!*

CHAPTER 3

I have always depended on the kindness of strangers.
—*A Streetcar Named Desire* (1951)

Herman's directions to the school proved to be accurate. The three-story brick building was at least a hundred years old. The sturdy school had large vertical windows, a bell tower on top, and at least a dozen steps to get into the large double front door.

I guess Little Beaver doesn't cater to the handicapped, Gen thought. *I'll wait until tomorrow to explore it.*

The Bumblebee Inn was across the street from the school's front entrance. *Great, I don't have to worry about driving to school in the morning.*

Gen stopped her car on the gravel road in front of the inn, which was partially hidden by a very large jack pine evergreen. The old house, like the school, had seen better days. The two-story structure, with many added-on porches and sheds, needed paint—badly. The black shutters hanging on either side of every window were old and worn. Several were hanging crooked because they needed to be fastened more securely.

Gen walked up to the front door and knocked.

No answer.

She knocked harder and shouted, "Anyone home?"

Gen saw the peephole at the top of the door open; an eye appeared. First the eye looked one way, then it looked the opposite way, and then it wandered around like it was searching for something. The deadbolt lock clicked, and the door squeaked open; it needed oiling.

A young man in his late twenties stood and stared at Gen. He was tall and lean and had a thin oval face, framed by thick, well-groomed light-brown hair. He would have been considered handsome if not for the eye defect.

His wandering eye examined Gen closely. With a childish grin on his face, he said, "You're even prettier than Miss Evie was."

"Oh—ah, thanks," Gen said. "I'm Gen Fletcher—and you are?"

He was silent for a moment like he didn't understand the question; then he perked up like something had finally registered in his brain. "I'm Benny Jacobs. My mom runs this place. She's having coffee with Mrs. Jacobear across the street. She left me in charge."

"Good—okay—can you help me bring in my things?"

"Yah," Benny answered and then propped the front door open and followed Gen to the car.

Gen loaded Benny up like a pack horse. She took the rest of the things that needed to be moved right away and followed Benny through the front door. She could come down later and get the rest of her things out of the trunk.

Benny talked all the while as he helped Gen. He had information on everything in sight, which included the grass, flowers, sidewalk condition, the house in general, and anything else that came to his mind.

They entered a small built-on shed that led to a hallway before entering the dining room. A steep flight of stairs was on the right side of the hall. The stairs were similar to those in many old houses: small, narrow, and steep. At the top of the stairs was a long hallway with a large bathroom (door open) in the center and a bedroom at either end.

"You'll share the bathroom with Oscar," Benny announced nonchalantly. "This here room is yours," he said, entering a spacious, clean bedroom with a large bed, dresser, chest of drawers, desk with a matching chair, and a closet with sliding doors.

"This is very nice," Gen commented.

"Mom takes good care of it," Benny said with a grin. He seemed to be very proud of his mom's housekeeping skills.

Benny put Gen's things gently on her bed and exited like he was embarrassed to be in a bedroom with a woman. "I'll be downstairs if you need anything," he said.

While Gen hung up her clothes and put away her other things, she wondered what Oscar was like. *I'll ask Benny later; he seems to be full of trivial information.*

About an hour later, she checked out the bathroom and then descended the steep stairway. She could hear a loud TV playing in Oscar's room.

The large arched opening across from the stairs led to the living room. Each room was separated by short side walls, about two feet high, that had Greek columns going the rest of the way to the ceiling. The kitchen was accessible through a set of swinging doors off the dining room; very open and comfortable looking. She walked out to the kitchen and saw a petite woman cooking on an electric stove. Her short, curly gray hair was peppered with traces of brown.

"Hello," Gen said.

No answer.

"Hello," Gen said louder as she walked up behind the woman and touched her on the shoulder.

The woman jumped and caught her breath as she turned around with her hands on her chest. "You scared me half to death," she said.

"Sorry, I thought you heard me. I said hello."

"I'm pretty deaf. See, I wear a hearing aid," she said, pointing to her ear, "but I don't always have it turned on." She smiled. "You must be Gen Fletcher, my new boarder?"

"Yes," Gen stuck out her hand as Mrs. Jacobs grabbed her and gave her a big hug.

"We're informal around here—just one big happy family," the landlady said with a chuckle. Her beautiful smile and friendly, sparkling eyes helped Gen warm up to her immediately.

Benny entered the kitchen.

"You've met my son, Benny. He helps me run this place. His twin brother, Bernie, lives in St. Paul; he's a dentist. He helps Benny and me out financially at times. I don't make much running a small boarding house in this town. Benny also does odd jobs around town, like mowing, snow shoveling, and such. We manage, dontcha know."

Gen waited for her to continue, but she didn't. There was an awkward pause.

Mrs. Jacobs broke the silence. "Benny will show you around the place—he likes to do that—then we'll eat. You probably want to get to bed early. You've had a long drive; tires a person out."

Benny was heading to the back shed, off the kitchen door. He beckoned Gen to follow him. At the foot of the back outdoor stairs was a flowerbed that had been freshly dug. It was about six feet square.

"We'll be planting lots of flowers here. Mom loves flowers; so did Miss Evie. She was a nice lady. She liked me."

Gen nodded.

The yard looked pretty dead except for the green grass that was growing between the dug-up patches of earth. Several of the trees were starting to leaf out, and the evergreens were looking very good. Some of the freshly dug earth was piled up in large mounds about a foot higher than the surrounding grass.

"Why is the ground so high in some places?" Gen asked.

"We plant veggies there. We use lots of fertilizer—saves on space. We also put a plastic fence around the patches later, after we get them planted," Benny explained. He seemed to know something about gardening and was very eager to share his knowledge.

After the yard tour, Benny took Gen into the house through the front door. He stopped at each item in the room and explained where it had come from. He seemed to have his tour-guide speech well rehearsed.

"This rocking chair was my grandma Mabel's. She rocked my mom in it."

"What is your mom's name?" Gen asked.

"Mom!" Benny answered with a puzzled look on his face.

"I mean her birth name—her given name."

"Oh." Benny giggled. "Marva."

Gen smiled. "That's pretty—and different."

Benny continued with his tour presentation. "This is a picture of our family when Bernie and I were little kids, with Mom and Dad."

"Where is your dad now?" Gen asked, examining the picture.

"Gone."

"What do you mean gone—like dead?"

"No, just gone. He left when Bernie and I were little and never came back."

"Oh," Gen said softly. *How sad*, she thought.

Benny went on to explain the wall hangings, furniture, family pictures, and a variety of crafted items. It took a long time to get around the room; there were lots of items to talk about.

"Supper's ready," Marva announced while putting the finishing touches on the dining room table. "You'd better call Oscar down, Benny."

Benny scurried over to the stairs and called, "Oscar, supper!"

Soon a fifty-something, well-groomed, slender man of average height, with dyed, thinning brown hair, came down the staircase. He stopped and stared at Gen. "Well, now, I see our new teacher has arrived. I was watching TV. I didn't hear you come in. I'm Oscar Olson. I teach math and science at the high school."

He stuck out his hand, and Gen shook it. "Glad to meet you, Oscar. I hope you can show me the school tomorrow. I'd like to see my room and supplies before Monday morning if possible."

"Sure thing. I have a key for the school. You'll get one too from Superintendent Gray when he gets here. He is in charge of several schools in the county, so he isn't at our school every day. Principal Haugen will show you the ropes."

"Sounds good," Gen said with a sigh of relief. *At least I don't have to hunt down a janitor to get into the school tomorrow. Things are working out great.*

Supper was delicious—chicken and dumplings. The obligatory conversation was casual and folksy. Gen learned about the school and its faculty from Oscar. She learned about the ladies' organizations in town from Marva, especially the church programs.

Benny sat quietly and ate. He seemed very childlike in his mannerisms and didn't seem to have anything to talk about at the supper table.

After supper Marva and Oscar offered to play three-handed pinochle with Gen, but she declined. "Some other night. I'm bushed. Doesn't Benny play pinochle?" she asked.

"Yes, I do!" Benny answered quickly like he'd been insulted. "But I'm busy tonight." He got up and left the room.

Gen looked at Marva and then at Oscar, wondering what she'd said to offend Benny.

Marva smiled. "It's okay, hon. Benny can get upset easily. He's playing computer games with a friend tonight." She got up and began clearing the table. Oscar helped.

Gen went upstairs to her room, took out her cell phone, and called her husband. *He should be home from work by now,* she reasoned.

The phone rang once, and Fletch answered. "Hello, sweetheart. What's the wild north like?" he teased.

"Well, you were right about the roads and conditions of the buildings, but the people are very friendly and helpful. I've been pleasantly surprised."

"Good. Does your room have indoor plumbing?"

"Don't be cute, smarty pants! Of course there is indoor plumbing. I share a bathroom with the other boarder, Oscar. He's the math and science teacher here."

"I hope he isn't tall, dark, and handsome."

"No, he's just a well-groomed and proper middle-aged man."

"Good. I don't need any rugged young men hanging around my girl."

Gen didn't tell him about Benny. She'd discuss him later when she knew more about him.

"How did work go today? Did you get that raise you were expecting?"

"Same old, same old. According to my boss, the sky is falling in the banking business." Fletch went on to discuss some problem he'd had with a bank customer. She listened patiently and then told him about her encounter with the elder men's coffee club.

There was a slight pause in the conversation. "I miss you already, sweetheart," Gen said.

"Good." He laughed. "Don't forget who you belong to."

"I won't." Gen yawned. "I'm so tired. Long drive today. I'll call tomorrow afternoon after I see the school. I'll give you a full report on my new working conditions."

"Okay. Bye, sugar babe."

"Good night, sweetheart." She hung up.

Why didn't I mention my encounter with Paul Bunyan? she thought. *Oh well, I guess it's not important.*

CHAPTER 4

How can we be expected to teach children how to
learn if they can't even fit inside the building?
—*Zoolander* (2001)

The sun streaming into her east bedroom window woke Gen up. For a moment she didn't know where she was. *What time is it anyway? I slept like a baby. All this fresh northern Minnesota air put me out for the night.*

The cracks between the curtains and shades on the window let in more light than Gen wanted. She'd have to ask Marva to fix that sometime.

She could smell something baking—caramel rolls, maybe? What a treat. She hadn't had fresh caramel rolls for breakfast since her last visit to the farm. Her mother made them often as a treat on Sunday mornings.

Grabbing her fuzzy, warm bathrobe, she started down the stairs.

"I hope I'm not late," she said to Marva, who was standing by the kitchen counter, surrounded by pans full of buns and rolls ready to bake. "What time is it anyway?"

"It's only eight. I thought I'd let you sleep in. Oscar and Benny went to the early service at the church. I thought I'd stay home and bake these. I hope you like caramel rolls."

"I love caramel rolls!" Gen said emphatically.

"Good. Coffee's ready over there." Marva pointed to the twelve-cup electric coffeemaker on the counter.

"Ummm," Gen purred, sipping her coffee and eating her caramel roll. "I think I died and went to heaven—pinch me, please." Then she thoughtfully added, "This must be a lot of work for you."

Marva laughed. "I make overnight bun dough, so all I had to do this morning was bake everything. The work started last night about eight when we made the dough. Oscar helped. He likes to cook. He often helps me with meals. By the way, if you ever want to cook anything, feel free to use my kitchen. Heaven knows that's what it's here for, dontcha know."

"Thanks," Gen said. She wasn't much for cooking and wasn't any good at it either.

Gen had detected a slight Scandinavian accent when Marva talked. "Are you Norwegian by any chance?"

Marva laughed. "You figured it out. Yes, I'm full blooded, and my husband was half. There are a lot of us mixed-blood people around here. Mostly Scandinavian, Chippewa or Ojibwa, and French Canadian.

Over a second cup of coffee and another roll, Gen learned about the French-Canadian fur traders who had intermarried with the Chippewa and Ojibwa in the mid-eighteenth century, and then the Scandinavian lumberjacks had come and intermarried with the offspring of the first intermarriages.

"We also have some Irish, English, and German blood around here—one big melting pot of humanity. We manage to get along most of the time," Marva said with a laugh as she put her last pan of buns into the oven to bake.

When Oscar and Benny got home from church, Gen made arrangements to go over to the school before lunch. She bounded up the stairs two at a time to get dressed. She was anxious to see her new workplace. As she hustled down the hallway, she noticed the small door on her left was slightly open.

"Hmm," she muttered. *I wonder who opened that door.* She stopped a moment to peep inside. She had thought before that it was a storage closet, but she was surprised to see it led to an attic up another flight of steep stairs. *Very interesting. I'll have to explore this later when I have more time.*

* * *

Oscar fumbled with the keys as he opened the small door on the west side of the school. "This is the staff entrance. The big front doors need a special key. Only the janitor, principal, and superintendent have that key," he informed Gen.

The door opened to a small platform that led down a short flight of stairs into the janitor's room. It was cozy and warm because the big coal furnace was located there. The entire school was heated with coal that heated water that turned to steam that ran in pipes and came out of the old-fashioned radiators as heat. It was a cheap way to heat the building but not too clean, Oscar informed her.

The building looked large from the outside, but the rooms were smaller inside. Grades one through four were located on the first floor. The wide-open staircase went up the middle of the building and led to the second floor, where grades five through eight were located. The large staircase then led to the third floor, where the high school was located. Each floor had four rooms. The large open area in the middle of the school took up a lot of room, but students could go from room to room and floor to floor very easily. You could see the first floor from the third floor by looking down the open staircase. This was kind of neat but took a lot of space away from each room.

Oscar chuckled. "I guess you could say that students in this school literally go higher and higher in their educational pursuits—if they keep passing."

"I see that." Gen looked troubled. "They not only have to get cognitively smarter, they have to get physically stronger to move up on this educational ladder. How do the handicapped survive?"

"Right now we don't have any physically handicapped in our school, although we do have some special education students," Oscar informed Gen. "There is an elevator built onto the school in the back of the building that will accommodate the physically handicapped. I'm not even sure if it still works. We haven't had handicapped people here for some time. Students and faculty are not allowed to use the elevator except in emergencies. We are encouraged to use the stairs for exercise."

The rooms are small, the building is old and not suited for the handicapped, Gen thought. *I wonder what the high school library and science rooms look like.* Her vision of a fine educational facility was fading.

The science room—to her surprise—had four very modern lab stations and was also used as the sophomore homeroom. This was Oscar's domain.

The library consisted of a wall full of book shelves that housed a large number of novels, classic and modern. The reference part of the library consisted of a globe, a large dictionary, two sets of encyclopedias, a variety of magazines, and several newspapers that were housed along the bottom of the huge vertical windows. Five new computers sat at the back of the room for students to do research. The library was also used as the freshman homeroom and study hall. It was the largest of all the high school rooms. The remaining two rooms housed the juniors and seniors and held classes in history, English, business, and a number of other social-science subjects. The English room, which was Gen's room, was also the senior homeroom. Oscar next informed her that she was also the new senior advisor.

At the back of the senior room were twelve new computers to help students do research and type papers. Gen could see that the bookshelves along the back of the room housed famous classical literature such as *To Kill a Mockingbird* and *The Sun Also*

Rises. There should be enough books for everyone in the class, Gen thought.

The history room contained textbooks for US history, European history, psychology, economics, government, and sociology. There were also social-science reference books and biographies of famous people.

Nestled between the four large rooms were smaller rooms that were used for the principal's office, teachers' lounge, and human-services people who visited the school on scheduled days and times. The girls' and boys' bathrooms were at the end of the wide-open hallway, between the rooms. The whole school was cozy, to say the least.

"I guess everyone knows everyone else here," Gen said with some semblance of hope.

"You might say that," Oscar chuckled. "We don't have students falling through the cracks here because of a lack of communication among the faculty. All of the faculty, grades one through twelve, share the teachers' lounge and work together on a variety of projects. We have to arrange a schedule each week that works for the entire school, since we share the gym and special-resource people. This place is like how the old-fashioned country schools used to be—where everyone was in one building and the older kids helped the little kids learn. We have high school students that tutor younger children in their spare time. We only have about 150 students in the entire school, and we have fourteen full-time faculty, a principal that also teaches some classes, and five special-programs teachers that come and go on different days. Our student/teacher ratio is about ten to one."

Not bad, Gen thought. *At least I won't have to correct fifty final research papers in senior English.*

Next Oscar took Gen down to the basement and out a side door that led to a hallway to the newer, state-of-the-art gymnasium. This building had been added on to the school about fifty years ago. The newer building contained the lunchroom, music room, and bathroom facilities.

"You can see where the community priorities are," Oscar said. "We do have good athletes here, especially football, basketball, and track. We've started to cooperate with some of the neighboring schools in the county in football and track. There just aren't enough students to fill all the positions."

"Well," Gen said wistfully when the tour was completed, "it looks like all the bases are covered, and if it's all well organized, it should work. If there is good community support and parental guidance, we should be okay. At least I won't get lost in the building the first day; it's mostly up and down. And if I get hungry, I go to the gym."

"That's right," Oscar said. "We do have excellent cooks, and they usually have a special treat for the faculty each day. It pays to be in good standing with the cooks."

* * *

That night when Gen relayed the content of her school visit to Fletch, she was upbeat and excited. "It's all so cozy, like a big old country school. I think it's a great place for me to start my teaching career."

"I'm glad you like it, sweetheart," Fletch responded. "Now don't get too friendly with the students. That can lead to discipline problems." Then he went on to tell Gen about an overly friendly teacher he had in high school who was eventually run out of the school by the kids.

"I know, don't smile for the first six weeks. Since I will only be here six weeks, I won't ever smile in front of the kids." Gen smiled to herself, thinking it might be her last time.

"I'm excited to meet the rest of the faculty," she continued. "Oscar sure seems nice. He told me that Evie wasn't very happy here. I wonder why not. I'll have to ask around and see if I can find out what happened with her. I don't want to make the same mistakes."

Fletch was very supportive. "I'm sure you won't. You're always such a positive person and not an airhead like Evie was. I'm sure you'll have a good experience."

The conversation continued in an upbeat fashion until they said their good nights. Then the room became eerily silent.

"It's lonely without Fletch," Gen said out loud. "Everyone else must be asleep—it's so quiet." She was talking to herself just to hear a human voice and break the silence.

The hinges on a door squeaked outside her room. She froze. *Maybe the wind is blowing the attic door open?* she thought. *Don't be silly. The Jacobses have a right to go up into their own attic whenever they want.* She had read too many novels about maniacs and secrets being locked up in the attics of old houses. That's all she could think of—what deep, dark secrets might be stored in the attic.

Gen grabbed the novel she'd been reading from her desk and opened it to page twenty-six. The mystery kept her occupied for about an hour; then she heard the squeaking door again. This time she also heard faint footsteps descending the stairs to the living room. *It was one of the Jacobses. What in the world were they doing in the attic for an hour?*

CHAPTER 5

Fasten your seat belts. It's going to be a bumpy night.
—*All About Eve* (1950)

Oscar walked Gen to the school on Monday morning and took her directly to the teachers' lounge to meet the rest of the faculty.

The first person she met was the physical education and business teacher. The tall, rugged, well-built, fortyish man was friendly and welcoming. He was at the school early most mornings, working with athletes in the weight room.

"Glad to have you aboard, Gen," he said. "I'm Nickolas Murrey—call me Nick."

"Hi, Nick, glad to meet you. I hear there are some very good athletes in this school."

"Yah," Nick said modestly. "We try."

Next came the art and music teacher, Miss Sailor—prim, proper, and single. She had that creative look about her.

"Nice to meet you, Gen." Miss Sailor had a plastered-on smile as she spoke. She looked like a fragile, frightened kitten. "I hope you like it here," she added without much enthusiasm. "I can't stay and chat. I've got a private lesson with one of the band students." With that comment, she left the room.

Poor thing, Gen thought, *she looks pretty beaten up.*

The next group, entering en masse, was the elementary faculty. Except for one middle-aged male, the other seven looked and talked like they could all have been made from the same mold. They were all local married women who had been there for many years. They were friendly, spoke in simple sentences, like they were in their classrooms speaking to their students, and dressed very professionally. All had generous body frames. It was plain to see that they played the roles of eager yet stern teachers, ready to shape young minds. The male was the eighth-grade teacher. He too had a mild manner and reminded Gen of TV's Mr. Rogers. After some obligatory chatter, the elementary entourage left in a group, the same way they had entered.

The principal, Mr. Haugen, wandered in, spotted Gen, and came over to introduce himself. He was average height, average looking, with a pompous air about him.

"So happy to have you aboard. Miss Pretsler left a gap that our faculty and substitute teachers have been trying to fill since she disappeared. Everyone will be happy to know you're here to take her workload. I'm sure the students will be happy too."

He grabbed a cup, filled it with coffee, and continued with instructions. "When you're done with your coffee, Mrs. Fletcher, please come to my office. I'll give you Evelyn's teaching books and other materials that she left behind. Her desk, in the senior room, has most of her other teaching supplies in it."

Mr. Haugen left the room with his coffee and air of importance. He undoubtedly had many important things to attend to.

I'm sure he'll have more instructions for me in his office, Gen thought. *I sure hope he does. I have some questions for him.*

The door flew open, and a tall, thin, wiry, thirty-something woman entered. Her blazing red hair was sticking out in all directions. She looked wildly around on the counter for a special cup.

Gen sat quietly, watching her scurry about like an agitated gerbil penned up in a cage. When she found the special cup, she filled it with coffee, sat down, and drank quickly.

After she had drunk about half the coffee, she seemed to calm down. Then she spied Gen sitting in the corner, visiting with Oscar and Nick.

"Oh my God!" she exclaimed. "I didn't see you there." She snorted a laugh. "I had one of those weekends where you're not sure on Monday morning what you did all weekend. Ever have one of those?"

Gen nodded and smiled politely.

"Well, let me tell you—I'm glad to see you here. Evie was fun, but that girl was short a few bricks from a full load. I always thought she'd disappear someday, and by God, I was right. Talk about an airhead."

Gen laughed. There was something likeable about this redhead. Whatever she was doing or saying looked and sounded crazy, but it all seemed to be natural.

"I suppose you're Mrs. Fletcher?"

"Yes, call me Gen."

"Gen, I'm Mildred Strutts. Miss Strutts to the kids and Millie to everyone else. I teach English, history, and speech. I'm running late, but I'll catch up with you at lunch, and we'll do some girl talk." She winked at Gen and then burst out of the lounge the same way she'd entered—like a small hurricane.

Oscar and Nick shook their heads. "Now you've met our Miss Strutts," Nick said. "She's a character, but the kids like her. She's funny but firm and knows her stuff. She doesn't take any BS from her students. The kids respect that."

"I'm sure they do," Gen said.

"Remember where your room is?" Oscar asked.

"Yes."

"Good. I've got to go. See you at lunch. Good luck."

Gen followed Oscar out of the lounge and went to the principal's office, circumventing the curious students in the hall. The principal was talking to a student with the door open. Gen waited until the student came out of the small office before entering.

"Have a seat, Mrs. Fletcher," Principal Haugen said very professionally.

Gen sat down in the chair the student had just vacated. Above Haugen's desk was a sign that read: *Teenagers: Tired of being harassed by your stupid parents and teachers? Act now! Move out, get a job, pay your own bills while you still know everything.*

Gen pointed to the sign. "A little bit of sarcasm?" She laughed.

Haugen smiled indulgently. He handed her some teacher's books, papers, and a daily schedule. "I think you'll find everything you need here. If not, I'm available every period of the day except 1:00 to 1:45. I teach psychology then. I'm also the school counselor if you need to refer students. In this school there is no breakdown in communication between the counselor and principal."

Gen glanced at the material she had been handed. "There's only a week's lesson plans here and no grade book," she said.

"Well, that's all I keep in my office. Everything else should be in Miss Pretsler's room or at her boarding place. She would normally hand everything in at the end of the school term."

"Okay." Gen paused. "I have a question. What if the students ask me about Miss Pretsler? What do I tell them?"

"Just tell them she resigned and won't be back."

"Isn't that a lie?"

"Well, yes, but since nobody knows what really happened to her, it's best we don't upset the students with all kinds of scary scenarios. Off the record, I think there was foul play. Miss Pretsler was a rather wild young lady and ran around with all kinds of local men. I think one of them did her in, but then, what do I know? The county sheriff won't tell me anything except that he is investigating the case."

Gen nodded while glancing at her schedule. "I think my whole day is outlined on the schedule. Oscar gave me a tour of the school yesterday, so I should be okay."

Haugen nodded and smiled.

Gen left, crossed the hall, and entered her room, where several students were already seated.

"Good morning," she said very professionally.

"Good morning," the students answered in unison, staring at their new teacher.

The students, two females and one male, had dark hair and eyes. Gen had been told the majority of her students would be a mixture of French Canadians, Native Americans, and dark Norwegians.

She sat down at her desk and looked through her books and other materials. The school buzzer sounded, and the seniors began to file into the room. There were twelve in all: seven girls and five boys. Several of the male students looked older than normal; she suspected they had been held back a grade or two somewhere along the line.

The students sat silently, emotionless, waiting for her to make the first move.

Gen cleared her throat and stood up. "I'm Mrs. Fletcher. I'll be your new English teacher the rest of the year. I'll also have you for government and civics. I hope we can complete the year on a positive note." She glanced around the room, looking for some emotional response, but received none. "Since I don't know any of you, I'm going to seat you in alphabetical order until I know your names."

There was a soft groan from the students.

"This seating arrangement will last until I know you; then we may make other arrangements."

This earned a sigh of relief from the room.

Gen called their names and seated all twelve, from Jim Anderson to Darrel Wanot, starting on the left side of the room.

The rest of the period consisted of Gen asking questions about where the students were in their English textbooks, what papers and projects they had completed this year, if there were any outstanding assignments and papers that were due soon, and what they felt might benefit them as seniors for the remainder of the school year. Several students were willing to give some limited information; most sat stone-faced and reluctant.

She discussed general punctuation and then gave a writing assignment. "I'd like to see what you know about punctuation; then we'll work on what you need help with," Gen said.

The students sat quietly, without expression. Gen wasn't sure they understood what the assignment was. No one asked questions.

When the buzzer sounded, the entourage got up and headed for their next destination, though she hadn't dismissed them. They were trained like Pavlov's dogs to respond to a buzzer.

I'd better be done when that buzzer sounds, because they will be out of here, come hell or high water, she thought.

The next class was junior United States history and then senior government. Those classes proceeded in the same fashion as senior English had. It seemed that all the students were programmed to be quiet, lack enthusiasm, and wait patiently to see what the new teacher was like.

At least they're predictable, she thought. *I'll have to ask someone about this type of behavior. Maybe this is the norm.*

When the buzzer sounded for lunch, she followed her students down the hallway into the gym. It smelled lovely—homemade buns, hamburger hotdish, fruit salad, bread, and milk. There was also a salad bar for those who didn't want the regular meal. No one ate the salad bar, so Gen took a plate and fixed herself a salad. It all looked so good; it was hard to choose.

Gen noticed several high school teachers sitting by themselves at a table. She went over to where they were seated and sat down.

Nick looked at her plate. "You can take both the hotdish and salad if you like," he said.

"Thanks. I'll eat this first and see if I need the hotdish too. I don't want to get fat. Once on the lips, forever on the hips."

Everyone laughed.

There was much chatter as the faculty ate—mostly about students, classes, and what had happened that morning. Gen thought the chatter was probably the same type of conversation the faculty had every day at lunch. It was all new to her but old to the rest. She listened and learned.

"Are the students always so quiet and lacking enthusiasm?" Gen asked.

Everyone laughed.

"I gave them assignments. Do you think they'll do them?" Gen asked.

"Maybe," Oscar said. "If they don't, give them a failing grade tomorrow and another assignment. Work with the students who hand in their work. The rest will get the idea after a while. Some just like to test you, to see if you'll buckle under."

Everyone nodded.

Gen went back to her room after lunch and checked out her junior English book. She had a study hall with fifteen people in it right after lunch; then came junior English. She'd have time to review her English assignment during study hall.

During junior English, the students hadn't changed their demeanor from the morning classes, so everything proceeded in the same fashion as before.

From 2:30 to 3:15, Gen had a group of eight remedial reading students who were deficient in their reading, writing, and comprehension skills.

This group consisted of ninth- through twelfth-grade students. Each had a different skill level, so all of them had different books and assignments. Gen talked to each student separately, to find out how they were progressing with their assignments.

Gen decided she didn't have enough time to work with each student separately, so she had each person choose a reading buddy, so they could work as a team. This would be a contest to see which team would improve the most in the next six weeks. She would be the judge. She would also give each pair ten minutes of her time per day, to help them with questions and instructions. The group seemed to like the competition idea. She gave them instructions and rules to follow. Then the buzzer sounded, and they were off.

"Whoosh." She let out a puff of air and a sigh of relief as the last student exited the room. "What a day!"

Gen got out her record book and recorded her day's progress. She recorded notes for each class, like a diary. This record would help her evaluate her progress each day. As she was finishing up, Millie appeared in the open doorway.

"How about a beer at the local watering hole before supper?" Millie asked.

"Sure," Gen said. "I need to ask someone a lot of questions, and that beer sounds good too."

CHAPTER 6

Here's looking at you, kid.
—*Casablanca* (1942)

The Coffee and Beer Cafe was almost deserted except for a short, wide man seated on a bar stool.

The ladies took a small table and patiently waited for a waiter to appear. Ed, as usual, was nowhere in sight.

"I'd swear that Ed hides out in back most of the time," Millie said.

"I've noticed he's not too ambitious. But since he runs the whole place, he's probably busy doing something else. We need to give him the benefit of the doubt," Gen said.

"Ladies out here!" the man at the bar shouted to no one in particular. He'd noticed the teaching duo enter the room by looking at the mirror behind the bar.

Millie snorted a laugh. "I guess we've been formally announced."

Shortly after the announcement, Ed appeared through a swinging side door next to the bar.

"Sorry, ladies, I didn't realize you were out here. What can I do for you?"

"I'll have a large, light, tap beer," Millie said and looked at Gen.

"Me too," Gen said.

Ed walked behind the bar to get the drinks.

"Who's that old geezer on the bar stool?" Gen asked.

"Charlie. He's the local barfly—lives in this place."

"Doesn't he work?"

"No. He got injured in the Vietnam War and gets a government check and social security. That's what he lives on. He does odd jobs around town when he's asked. He'll be over to greet us soon. He hits on me every once in a while when I come into this bar. He thinks I'm one of the local floozies." Millie laughed.

"Here he comes!" Gen warned, while Millie muffled her laughter.

Charlie got up from the bar stool and adjusted the belt on his waistband, which was hiding beneath his beer belly. He was also wearing suspenders that were connected to his blue jeans and ran up the front of his long-sleeved, blue-and-green plaid shirt. His whole outfit—including him—could have used some cleaning.

"Afternoon, ladies. I see you have a new friend, Millie." He introduced himself. "I'm Charlie McCann." Charlie gave Gen his best, sexiest toothless grin.

Millie smiled. "Hello, Charlie. Glad to see you're out and about. This is our new teacher, Gen Fletcher."

"Hello, Miss Fletcher." Charlie stuck out his hand.

Gen took the hand and shook it reluctantly. *God only knows where that hand has been*, she thought. "Nice to meet you, Mr. McCann."

"Call me Charlie." He grinned.

"Call me Gen. I hear you were in the Vietnam War. Thank you for your service."

Charlie nodded modestly. He didn't have any comments to make.

Millie changed the subject. "How's everything going for you, Charlie?"

"Well, you know, I have my good days and bad days. My left leg swells now and then—a real bummer." He paused a second. "A war injury, dontcha know," he added sadly.

"Sorry to hear that," Gen said.

Ed appeared with the beer. He looked at Charlie. "Charlie, leave these ladies alone to relax after a hard day's work."

Charlie grumbled and went back to his bar stool. Ed disappeared behind the swinging doors.

"Charlie's okay," Millie said, "just lonely."

"Yeah, I guess."

"Now, what did you want to ask me?"

Gen fired one question after another at Millie. She asked about school rules and regulations. Millie filled her in on the written rules and the implied rules that were present in most schools. For example: you call everyone Miss, Mister, or Missus. That was implied, not written down on paper. And you stay after school is out for at least half an hour; that was written in your contract.

"Evie's records for the year seem to have disappeared. Haugen only gave me lesson plans for the week of April first through the fifth, the week after she disappeared. Where do you suppose her other records are?" Gen asked.

"Who knows? Evie wasn't too organized. Neither is Haugen. Between the two of them, they've probably lost all her past records."

Gen nodded and began asking questions about some of the students who seemed to be the class leaders.

Millie gave her opinions and then stated that Gen should find out for herself what each student was like and not judge them by what others said.

Last, she asked about the faculty. "What's the story on Nick?"

"He's been here a long time. Seems to enjoy his job. He's married and has two grown kids. His wife quilts. She's the quilter from hell. She quilts for her family, the church, and to sell. I've seen her quilts. They're beautiful."

"Oh," Gen said. "What about Oscar?"

"Oscar is a very smart man and an excellent teacher. I don't know what he's doing in this school. He's good enough to teach anywhere in the state. Rumor has it he was running way from something when he came here. I've never asked him about it; he's very private. I always think 'live and let live.' Keep your nose out of other people's business, and you'll be fine. Besides, I think he's got a crush on Marva. They are so cute together. He helps her cook."

"Yes, Marva told me. Well, if they like each other, that's great. Too many lonely people in the world," Gen mused.

There was a moment of silence. "I had an accident on the way here," Gen began. "I ran off the road to keep from hitting a deer. I ended up with part of my car in the ditch. This tall, good-looking guy—I call him Paul Bunyan—came along in an old red pickup and pulled me out."

Millie smiled. "I see you've met D.J."

"D.J. who?"

"Derek James Danson, our local stud. He's one hunk of a man with a big attitude problem."

"Tell me about him."

"Well, let's see. He was born and raised on a small farm about three miles northwest of town. His dad was a Scandinavian logger and his mother a princess—combination French Canadian and Chippewa. He has a sister named Liz. She's married to Carl Larson, who owns the convenience store."

"Oh, sure, I've met Liz—very attractive lady."

"Yah. Carl also logs about eight months of the year. He's gone right now and working for a lumber company near Duluth."

Millie paused a second and took a sip of her beer. Gen sat and waited for more information.

"D.J. went to school here—local hero, very good athlete. He set some high school records in football, basketball, and track that have never been broken. Funny thing about him being an outstanding athlete—he's also very intelligent. Graduated the top of his class. Got a full-ride scholarship to the University of Minnesota. He majored in business with minors in English literature and human science—weird combination. I guess he loves to read. He can quote Shakespeare like a pro. His looks and demeanor really throw you when he starts talking to you."

"You said he has a big attitude problem. Why?" Gen asked.

"He met a beautiful girl at the 'U' and married her. Brought her home to live on the farm. She hated it but put up with it for a while. D.J. was in the Minnesota National Guard. When the guard was called for duty during the Afghanistan war, D.J. went. When he got back, his wife was gone. She filed for a divorce and hasn't been back. I think she's remarried."

Millie paused for a second, reflecting on what to tell Gen next. "To me he seems to be bitter, resentful, overly proud, hurt—who knows. He doesn't say much about his life. He uses women. Don't get me wrong; he's not mean. A great lover—I know, I was one of his harem for a while. Then I decided it wasn't worth the heartache watching him cat around."

Gen looked at Millie with sympathy and thoughtfulness. *Why would an attractive, intelligent woman like Millie fall for a guy like that?*

As happy hour approached, more people entered the bar. Jack Beane and Jim Stern came in. They greeted Gen and Millie and then sat down at a small table near the bar and had a beer.

Two younger, dark-haired, dark-eyed women entered and took a small table in the farthest corner of the bar.

"What do you know about Evie's disappearance?" Gen asked Millie.

"Not much. I've told you what I thought of her. She used to come here with me. I don't know how she got home. I suppose one of the local Romeos took her home. She drank too much, in my opinion."

"Did D.J. ever date her?"

"I'm sure he did; he dates every single woman who shows up around here—also a few married ones. He doesn't discriminate in that respect. You know, if you really want to know something about Evie, go ask Charlie. He sits here most every night and sees lots of things. He's not as dumb as people think he is. After a few drinks, he likes to talk."

"Well, speak of the devil!" Millie was looking at the swinging entrance doors to the bar.

In walked Paul Bunyan, tall, proud, and handsome as ever. He meandered straight over to where the teaching duo was seated.

"Evening, ladies. Thought I might find you here. Gotten stuck lately?" he asked, looking at Gen.

"No."

"Good. Mind if I sit down?"

"No, suit yourself," Gen answered. Millie said nothing.

"How have you been?" he asked Millie.

"I'm good. Didn't know you were interested in my health," she answered sarcastically.

"Little feisty, are you?" He glared at Millie. She glared back.

"I wanted to thank you for pulling me out of the ditch on Saturday," Gen said, "but you left in such a hurry, I didn't have time. How about letting me buy you a beer?"

"Sure."

Gen motioned to Ed, who was sitting on a stool behind the bar. He strolled over to their table.

"Get D.J. a beer, please," Gen said to Ed. "Put it on my tab."

Ed shook his head indulgently. "She's only been in town three days and is buying you a beer already. How do you do it?"

D.J. grinned and shrugged.

"O-o-oh, you don't understand," Gen stuttered. "H-h-he did me a big favor. I'm just trying to be appreciative …"

"Don't have to explain, little lady," Ed said. "It happens all the time."

Millie touched Gen's arm. "It's okay, sweetie—we all understand," she said and snorted a laugh.

Gen slumped in her chair and became silent for a moment. Millie and D.J. talked about his horses and dogs. He raised Indian ponies and hunting dogs, all purebreds, to sell.

"I think I'll go talk to Charlie about you-know-what," Gen said to Millie.

"Sure."

Gen sat down beside Charlie on a bar stool. Charlie grinned his big, toothless grin, apparently happy someone wanted to talk to him.

"Millie tells me you are a good source of local gossip," Gen said.

"Sure," Charlie bragged, "not much escapes me, dontcha know."

"What can you tell me about Evie Pretsler? I was sort of a friend of hers in college. I'd like to hear your theory on her disappearance."

"I didn't get to know her too well. She was kind of flirty and maybe a little crazy. After a few drinks, she talked crazy—you know, kind of sent mixed messages and ideas. She went home most nights with one or another of the local single men. A few married men took her home too. Now, don't get me wrong. I'm no prude. What the men folks in this community do is their own business."

"Can you tell me which married men took her home?"

"Well, let me think." Charlie rubbed his balding head. "The banker, Elroy Hoffer, offered her a ride home once when she was very drunk, and Swen Swenson, a local farmer—he's married to a Chippewa woman—took her home a few times. They're both nice guys. Neither one would hurt a fly, dontcha know."

"Glad to hear that. What can you tell me about D.J.?"

Charlie smiled. "D.J. is our local hero. He's always made Little Beaver proud. He's smart—really smart. Uses all kinds of big, fancy words. Writes poetry, I hear. He's also a good athlete. He's kind of down on the world right now—doesn't like the war, politics, religion, but loves the ladies, his horses, and his dogs. Most of the ladies love him too." Charlie chuckled. "I wish I had his charm and good looks."

"Be careful what you wish for, Charlie." Gen patted Charlie's arm. "Trying to please all the ladies could become a regular chore and a little dangerous, if you know what I mean."

Charlie grinned and nodded.

"Do you suppose any of D.J's girlfriends could have gotten mad at him or Evie and caused some harm?"

"Naaah, I doubt it. We mostly get along here. Everyone understands the barroom protocol around here. Share and share alike, dontcha know." Charlie looked very serious and sure about his last statement.

"If you say so, Charlie. You know these people better than I do." Gen smiled and patted Charlie's arm again. "How *do* you know all this stuff?" she asked.

Charlie smiled. "I just sit here and watch and listen like a little mouse in the corner. Most people don't even notice me. They all think I'm too drunk to catch what they're saying."

"That right?" Gen smiled and motioned to Ed, who was standing nearby. "Ed, bring Charlie another beer, please, and put it on my tab." Then she got up off the bar stool and went back to the table where Millie was now sitting by herself.

D.J. had moved on and was now seated with the two young, dark-haired women in the far corner of the bar.

"Well, I see he's found a greener pasture to graze in," Gen said with a chuckle.

"I guess so," Millie agreed. "Want another beer?"

"No, thanks. One's my limit. Besides, I don't want to be late for supper after my first day of work. Marva is a good cook, and I'm starved."

CHAPTER 7

After all, tomorrow is another day!
—*Gone With the Wind* (1939)

After a delicious supper of pork chops and baked potatoes, Gen went to her room. She needed to call Fletch and tell him all about her day.

He answered the phone after only two rings. "Hi, sweetheart, how was your first day of school?"

"Fletch, it's so good to hear your voice. What a day this has been. Where do I start?"

Gen went on to tell all about meeting the faculty, talking to Principal Haugen, and her encounters with each class of students. She described Millie, Nick, Haugen, and Oscar in some detail, while the rest of the faculty she mentioned casually. She discussed her encounters with each of her classes in some detail and also expressed her disappointment with the students' lack of enthusiasm for anything she said or did.

"Don't worry about the kids," Fletch said. "I'm sure they'll come around. You need to be patient. With Evie for a teacher, they probably got away without doing anything. You'll have to be firm."

"I know. I'm just a bit apprehensive about the whole business. They seemed so bored with everything I said."

"You'll see. They'll warm up to you. Soon they'll all love you like I do." He chuckled.

"Thanks, Fletch. You always make me feel better."

Gen next told Fletch about her café/bar experience with Millie and the people she'd met there. She described Charlie as "a sweet, little old man who was lonely and drank too much." She described D.J. as "a womanizing chauvinist who thought he was God's gift to women."

Fletch remained quiet during her detailed discussion of Little Beaver's happy-hour social life. When she'd finished, he said, "Sounds like fun, but don't get too involved with those people. Remember, you're only there for six weeks."

Finally Gen discussed what she'd found out from the local residents about Evie. "Most think she just left. They think she was an airhead. The principal thinks there was foul play because Evie had a wild, promiscuous lifestyle. I think he's kind of a self-righteous hypocrite myself. The fact that she accepted rides home at night from married men worries me. Maybe some wife threatened her or did her harm. You know we married women can get testy when some other woman makes a move on our man."

Fletch laughed. "I'd hate to see you get testy. You can be pretty mean when you're mad."

"Yes, I can—so watch out." Gen laughed.

"If some woman did Evie in, the law would probably find a body someplace. A woman probably wouldn't be strong enough to move a body or take a dead body a long ways to bury it. She wouldn't have time. She'd be busy cooking and cleaning," Fletch surmised.

"That's awful," Gen replied. "You're talking about some slave. If a woman only did cooking and cleaning for her man, she'd probably thank Evie for stealing him and setting her free!"

The discussion continued and got more absurd as time went on. They finally said their good nights, and Gen found herself alone in her silent room. She got out the portable CD player she'd brought along and put on one of her favorite CDs, playing the music softly so she wouldn't disturb the rest of the people in the house. She read her mystery until she was very sleepy. Then she turned off the light and slipped into slumber.

* * *

Her fears were confirmed during her first-period class. When she asked the students to get out their homework assignments, only three, Dawn, Amanda, and Clint, had done the work. These students were the same three who had volunteered to give her information the day before. She went over their papers and discussed punctuation rules, to help the three make corrections in their assignment. The rest of the students sat quietly and looked bored.

At the end of the period, about five minutes before the buzzer sounded, Gen gave another assignment on capitalization. Then she said, "Since I will be giving daily grades on homework assignments and participation in class, the only three students who will get a grade today are those who handed in their assignments and participated in the discussion. The rest of you failed today. I hope you realize you need this credit in senior English to graduate."

The students looked mutinous as they sat silently glaring at their teacher.

Gen paused a moment, showing no fear. "You can work on your assignment for tomorrow until the buzzer sounds; then you are dismissed," she said calmly.

The three ambitious students went right to work. Three others watched for a moment; then they got out a sheet of paper and pencil and begin their assignment. The other six sat silently and waited for the buzzer.

The rest of the day's classes were similar to the first. A few had their assignments done, while the rest sat and watched. Gen followed the same firm but nonconfrontational style she had followed in her first class.

Her last period of special reading students went a little better. The students were happy to read to each other and use Gen as a source of information and instruction. When she came to each team's study area, she asked them questions about what they were reading. Gen engaged them in conversations about the story and encouraged them to give their opinions. She also encouraged them to challenge each other's opinions if they thought their interpretation was better than that of their study buddy.

Even the students who weren't good readers were capable of deducing meaning from their stories and expressing their ideas. The students seemed to enjoy their debates.

After school Gen went to Millie's room and told her what had happened in each class.

"They're testing you," Millie said. "Tomorrow you'll have a few more assignments turned in by those who don't want a failing grade the last six weeks. Maybe by the end of the week— with a little luck—they will all be doing their homework."

"I hope so. It's going to be a long six weeks if they don't," Gen sighed.

"Interested in another encounter with the before-supper social group?" Millie asked.

"No thanks. Marva is having supper a little earlier tonight. She's got a church women's group meeting tonight and has invited me to come along. I guess I'll go. Maybe if some of the ladies are mothers of my students, I can encourage them to talk to their kids about homework assignments."

"Sounds good, but don't hold your breath," Millie joked.

* * *

The ladies' social group at the church was 90 percent retired women, so Gen didn't impress too many with her enthusiasm for homework. However, her philosophy on diets seemed to impress some for a few moments.

Many of the ladies were overweight and had tried a variety of diets through the years. After the lesson about Christian faith was over, their favorite topics for discussion were diets and food, which were contradictory and caused a few tempers to flare.

Gertie Amen, who seemed to be the head of the fat police, was skinny as a rail, so she felt she knew more about dieting than anyone else. She watched each lady load her plate with sugary goodies that had been brought to share before, during, and after the meeting. If someone took more than one cookie or bar, Gertie turned her head in disgust. When one of the older ladies took three sweet delights, Gertie said, "You know all that sugar will kill you."

Annie Ryan, the oldest member of the society, answered, "So what? I'm eighty-eight years old, and something is going to kill me anyway. I'd rather die eating bars and cookies than smoking. It's cheaper!"

That shut Gertie up because—Gen found out later—she was a heavy smoker.

Marva, a natural peacemaker, tried to calm the waters by making a suggestion. "Since Gen is so slim and attractive, why don't we ask her what she thinks of diets?"

Everyone looked at Gen.

"Well—I-I ..." Gen stammered, "I'm not really into either sweets or dieting." She paused a moment to think of something diplomatic to say. "I believe in all things in moderation. I try to eat healthy and do firming, light exercise. 'Never sweat' is my motto."

Everyone stared at Gen. Some thought her 'everything in moderation' statement might be from the Bible. Women from both sides of the fence nodded in agreement.

Marva was pleased with Gen's answer. "Well, now," she said, "we seem to have a person in our midst who sees the value of eating things we enjoy, eating healthy, and exercising—a real compromise. Since Gen has shown wisdom in this respect, maybe she is also a good teacher. We should all encourage our children and grandchildren to listen to her instructions and learn something."

Gen was very grateful for Marva's compliment. Maybe some of the ladies would go home and encourage their children and grandchildren to listen to the new teacher.

Gen's advice didn't last too long. It must have fallen on stony ground. The conversations continued. When someone tasted a cookie or bar that was especially good, they found out who the donor was and asked for the recipe. The dieters sat stern faced, drinking their coffee and discussing exercise. Nothing much had changed.

Gen sat silently and observed the group. Mrs. Hoffer (Donna) and Mrs. Swenson (Angela) were part of the serious dieting group that was now discussing the use of pills to lose weight. Gen had heard of people on strict diets, especially those on pills, going berserk and whacking people. *Maybe one of them whacked Evie,* she thought. *They both had motives to do so. Evie was skinny as a rail, and if she had been messing around with their husbands, they probably lost it and did her in. Maybe it was a conspiracy.*

What a preposterous idea! Gen thought. *This detective work is making me crazy.*

"Are you ready to go?" Marva whispered to Gen as the social drew to a close.

"Sure am!" Gen said. She'd had enough of the food-versus-diet conversations.

CHAPTER 8

Louie, I think this is the beginning of a beautiful friendship.
—*Casablanca* (1942)

"It's hump day," Millie announced when she entered the teachers' lounge Wednesday morning. Her hair was in disarray, and she looked tired.

"Geez, Millie, don't you ever sleep at night?" Nick teased.

"I sleep! Actually, I was home early last night, but I had twenty written assignments to correct, so I didn't get to bed until after midnight."

"Can't you just count the number of pages and give those with the most pages As and the next-most pages Bs, and so on?" Nick suggested with a mischievous look on his face.

"No!" Millie said emphatically. "Only physical-education teachers get away with such grading tactics. I feel that when the students hand in assignments that took them a week to write, I owe them my best editing job and helpful comments for those assignments. That's my job. My social life may not always be school-board approved, but by God they can't criticize my teaching."

Gen looked at Nick and laughed. "I think you've gotten her dander up," she said.

Nick laughed. "I like to rattle her chain now and then. Actually, I like her beautiful hair when it's so nicely groomed."

"Humph!" Millie muttered and left the teachers' lounge in a huff.

"Now look what you've done," Oscar scolded Nick.

"Come on, guys, chill out!" Nick said as he got up and left.

Gen went to her room and began looking through every drawer and shelf for Evie's past records. She found nothing.

A few minutes later, Dawn Kingfish entered the room. She came up to Gen's desk and stood there silently with no sign of emotion.

The senior girl had the same features as all the mixed-blood students in the school. Her hair was dark and shiny, and she wore it long and straight. Her eyes were dark and lively. She had no body fat on her five-foot-eight-inch frame.

Gen had heard that Dawn was a good athlete. She had qualified for state competition in many running events on the school track team.

"What can I do for you, Dawn?" Gen asked.

"I-I-I'm having … I-It's just that I-I-I'm not sure … b-b-but …" Then Dawn shut her mouth and said no more.

Gen looked at the flustered young girl. "It's okay to ask for help, Dawn. That's what I'm here for."

Dawn stood silently, mulling over what Gen had said.

"Can I see your assignment for today?" Gen asked.

Dawn handed Gen her paper.

Gen studied the paper for a moment and then said, "This looks fine. We'll go over everyone's work in class."

Dawn took the paper and stood silently. She seemed to have a question but was hesitant to ask.

"Was there anything else?" Gen asked.

Dawn handed Gen another set of papers. After a quick look at them, Gen recognized them to be college registration forms. Gen smiled as she remembered all the forms she'd filled out for college. "Did you want help with these?" Gen asked.

Dawn nodded.

"Okay. Grab a chair and sit down. We'll work on these."

Gen started reading page one out loud. As she read each line of instructions and explained them to Dawn, the girl filled in the information. *Can't she read?* Gen thought. *She seems to understand what to do when I read it.*

After two pages of the procedure, Gen asked, "Can you read, Dawn?"

Dawn nodded.

"Then you read the next part of the form."

Dawn hesitated and then began. "F-f-fill i-i-in th-th-the—" She stopped reading.

"Do you have a stutter?" Gen asked.

Dawn nodded.

"That's okay. I'll read. Just remember, I don't care if you stutter. Your assignment yesterday was done very nicely, and today's seems fine too."

Gen touched Dawn's arm. "Are you working with the speech therapist who comes once a week?"

Dawn nodded.

"Good. I'm sure you'll conquer this."

The buzzer sounded, and the seniors began filing into the room.

"We'll finish this form after school, okay?" Gen asked.

Dawn nodded.

* * *

A few more students handed in assignments on Wednesday. Gen's spirits lifted. *Maybe they will all have assignments done by Friday.*

Responses and participation in classes were still scarce. *I'll have to try something new to encourage more class interaction,* Gen thought.

Gen's last period class was working fine. Students were interacting with each other and with her. *Maybe the answer is to put them into groups—to let them talk to each other. I'll try that tomorrow with all my classes.*

After school, Gen helped Dawn finish her registration forms. She spoke to Dawn about college and her own experiences. Dawn started speaking with a few crisp *yes, no,* and *maybe* answers. She seemed to handle small talk just fine when she could be brief.

When the girl left her room, Gen smiled to herself. *One word at a time*, she thought.

Millie stuck her head into Gen's room through the open door. "Time for a hump day refreshment?"

Gen smiled. "Okay. Let me gather up my homework and coat. I'll come over to your room."

"Good!" Millie disappeared.

* * *

Happy hour was in full swing when Gen and Millie arrived at the Coffee and Beer Café/Bar. It was an hour later than it had been on Monday. Charlie was sitting on his usual bar stool, and Elroy and Graywolfe were at a small table. Gen didn't know any of the other people in the café/bar. *Everyone must celebrate hump day in Little Beaver*, Gen thought.

The English teachers each ordered a beer from the waitress who was wandering around. While they were waiting for their beer, in walked Sheriff Martin Schultz, dressed in full law-enforcement uniform. He was short, overweight, clean shaven, and had an air of overconfidence.

Gen looked at Millie and laughed. "That's the law around here?"

"That's our local Nazi SS officer." Millie snorted a laugh. "He's single, if you're interested."

"No, thanks! Remember, I'm married. Do you think I'd step out on my husband?" Gen was incredulous.

Millie shrugged. "Doesn't matter to me what you do. Nights are cold and long up here. People have needs—"

"Forget it!" Gen said emphatically, shutting Millie off in midsentence.

"Okay! Don't get your panties in a knot. I'm very liberal—you know—to each her own. No pressure, hang loose, and all that sort of BS."

The sheriff looked around the bar, scrutinizing the place and the people. Then he spotted Gen and Millie. He strolled over to their table. "Good evening, ladies."

"Evening, Sheriff Schultz," Millie said. "This here is our new teacher, Mrs. Fletcher." Millie put extra emphasis on *Mrs.*

"Happy to make your acquaintance," Sheriff Schultz said as he stuck out his hand.

Gen shook the extended hand. "Likewise, I'm sure." Her voice sounded a little like Judy Holliday's in *Born Yesterday*.

The sheriff sat down at their table without being asked. He motioned to Ed. "The usual," he said when Ed was within earshot.

"How is the investigation into the disappearance of Evelyn Pretsler coming?" Gen asked.

The sheriff looked surprised. "Why do you want to know?" he asked.

"I knew her in college, and I'm replacing her here. I'd kind of like to know what my future is here. Maybe something bad will happen to me. Maybe people in Little Beaver don't like English teachers."

"I'm sure you have nothing to fear, Mrs. Fletcher. If people in Little Beaver didn't like English teachers, Millie would have been done in years ago." The sheriff let out a hearty laugh.

"I'm sure the excellent law enforcement in the area has saved me from such a fate," Millie said, sarcasm dripping from every word. The sheriff didn't catch the sarcasm, so he puffed out his chest and beamed at Millie's comment.

The waitress brought their drinks. The teachers paid her and tipped. The sheriff said, "Put mine on my tab."

"Well, what about the Evie Pretsler case?" Gen asked again.

"We're working on it. I can't divulge too much, dontcha know. I don't want to alert any guilty parties."

"Do you have any theories or new clues?" Gen persisted.

"No."

"Isn't it true that the longer you wait to solve a case, the less likely you are to ever solve the mystery?"

"Sometimes, but we haven't found a body yet or anything else that says there was foul play, so maybe we don't have a case," the sheriff replied in a firm tone of voice. He seemed to be getting a little irritated with Gen.

"Good deduction." Gen complimented the sheriff with a hint of amusement in her voice.

A know-it-all expression crossed his face, "Leave it to me, little lady. We'll get to the bottom of this sooner or later."

"We're all in your corner, Martin," Millie said with a touch of irony in her voice.

"Thanks, ladies. I think I'll talk to Charlie. He's my secret source of information, dontcha know."

When the sheriff was out of earshot, Millie leaned over to Gen. "Charlie is everybody's secret source of information, dontcha know." She snorted a laugh.

Gen giggled. *So this is how the law around here works.* She burst into full laughter. The more she thought about it, the more she laughed. Millie joined her. Laughter is good, even at the expense of the Little Beaver law department.

"What are you two laughing at?" D.J. asked. The teachers hadn't noticed him coming over to their table during their fit of laughter.

"None of your beeswax!" Millie said.

D.J. sat down uninvited. "The sheriff is a pompous ass," he said. "Thinks he knows everything."

"Takes one to know one!" Millie answered.

"Well, I guess I know when I'm not wanted," D.J. said, glaring at Millie.

"Clever boy!" Millie glared back.

D.J. got up and left.

"You're a little rude to him, aren't you?" Gen asked. "Are you sure you're not still in love with him?"

"I'm so over him!" Millie shot back.

"Sorry, it's none of my business, but you two sound just like a married couple who just got divorced and are still dealing with hurt feelings."

"Well, we were never married or even in a close relationship, but our so-called friendship has turned rotten. I can't put up with his arrogance now that I'm not sleeping with him. What a fool I was!"

"Oh, well," Gen sighed. "Dontcha know that a perfect relationship is when two imperfect people don't give up on each other?"

Millie shrugged, seeming uninterested in Gen's advice.

Gen paused a moment and glanced to where Charlie was sitting at the bar. The sheriff had moved on to get pertinent information from other secret sources. Gen decided to talk to Charlie; he probably knew more than the sheriff did.

"Do you mind if I go talk to Charlie?" she asked Millie.

"No, go right ahead. I want to talk to Lilly, the waitress, for a few minutes. I have her daughter in class and need to discuss something with her."

Gen walked over to where Charlie was seated. He saw her coming and gave her his best toothless grin. He was also sporting two days' growth of facial hair. *He must have forgotten to shave,* Gen thought, *or maybe he thinks that's sexy looking.*

"Hi, Charlie, how are things going?"

"Not bad," Charlie answered. "The sheriff was just here asking me things." He sat up straight and tall on his bar stool, indicating a sense of pride.

"Well now, you must know something important, to have a person as busy as the sheriff stop and talk to you."

"Yes, sirree!" Charlie said, puffing up is chest. "I found a cell phone in a ditch on the edge of town yesterday when I was picking up cans to sell. Pretty good money for cans now, dontcha know."

"A cell phone?" Gen was very interested. "Whose was it?"

"Well, I gave it to Sheriff Schultz last night. They examined it, and I guess it was Evie's. I wonder what it was doing in the ditch."

"Maybe she lost it on the way home one night," Gen speculated.

"Yah, maybe, or maybe her murderer discarded it," Charlie said with eyebrows raised and an intelligent look plastered on his face.

"What was on the phone?" Gen asked.

"The sheriff won't say. He said it might give information to the guilty party if it leaked out."

"The sheriff is right about that," Gen assured Charlie. "If you find out what was on the phone, I'd sure like to know." She winked at him, and he gave her the thumbs-up.

"Thanks, Charlie." Gen motioned to Ed. "A drink for my friend Charlie," she said and walked back to where Millie was once again seated all by herself.

"Any luck with Charlie?" Millie asked.

Gen smiled. "I think Charlie likes me and is going to be my secret source of information too."

A round of hearty giggling ensued as the teaching duo finished their beers and left.

CHAPTER 9

I'll be back!
—*The Terminator* (1984)

Thursday proved to be a fruitful day at school. In senior English, Gen had the students choose someone to work with and exchange their assignment for correction. Two students still didn't have their assignments done, so Gen put them together at the back of the room and told them they could work on their past assignments while the others corrected today's assignments.

The seniors did a good job of critiquing each other's work. They seemed to enjoy finding mistakes on their partner's paper. Gen noticed they weren't always discussing their English assignments. She could hear them talking about school activities and what they were planning for the weekend. *Even if they are not always on task*, Gen thought, *they are no longer sitting like zombies.*

Their final assignment for the week was "write a few short paragraphs about the most important things you've learned from your senior English assignments this year. You can also make English lesson suggestions for the remainder of the year." They were to use the grammar skills they had learned so far this week. This paper was to be short and concise.

When the buzzer rang, Dawn come up to thank Gen for her help with the college entrance forms.

"You're welcome. Have you mailed them yet?" Gen asked.

"Yes, th-th-this morning."

"Good. You're on your way. Anything else you need help with, let me know, okay?"

"Okay." Dawn smiled and left.

Gen's two history classes went better after she assigned groups of three to discuss issues that were presented in their history reading. The classrooms became louder as students argued the ramifications of some historical actions by people in power. *Spirited arguments are better than silence*, Gen thought. The open communication promoted opinions, which resulted in more learning in each class.

When the day ended, Gen had a feeling of accomplishment.

Millie appeared at Gen's open door at her usual time. "Ready for a refreshing beverage?" she asked.

"Not tonight," Gen said. "I promised Marva I'd play pinochle with her, Oscar, and Benny. I'll have to do my lesson plans and correct papers now, so I can take the night off. I also need to call my husband."

Millie nodded and smiled. "Did things go better today?"

"Yes, much better. There was some action in class for a change, and I didn't feel like I was giving a lecture all the time."

"Good. See you tomorrow morning in the lounge?"

"Sure, I'll be back, bright-eyed and bushy-tailed, ready for another day of fun!" Gen teased.

Millie laughed and left.

Gen finished her corrections and lesson plans for Friday, straightened up her desk, grabbed her coat, and went home.

The house was very quiet when Gen entered the front door. "Anybody here?" she called as she walked out to the kitchen.

There was silence.

A Crock-Pot full of beef stew was simmering on the kitchen counter. "Mmm, that smells good," Gen said.

I wonder where everyone is. Gen looked out the back door. *Nobody in the backyard either. That's strange; Oscar must have stayed late at school too.*

Then she remembered reading on the day's announcement sheet that Oscar was the coach of the Academic Pursuit Team that was practicing tonight after school for a contest on Saturday morning in Bemidji.

Gen went up the stairs to her room. She noticed the door at the end of the hallway was open. *This might be a good time to explore the attic*, she thought.

The staircase was narrow and steep. Gen climbed into the musty, foul-smelling attic. The big room was large enough to stand up and walk around in. The room was filled with boxes, trunks, and all kinds of old furniture. Old clothes were hanging on nails and rope lines stretched across the corners.

Wow, she thought, *some of these things are antiques—really neat stuff. Everything is dusty, and there are a lot of spider webs around here.*

There were dresses from the twenties, old armed-services uniforms from WWII, and the furniture dated back to the early 1900s. *This is a gold mine*, Gen thought. *I wonder why Marva keeps all this stuff hidden.*

Gen noticed a trunk that had been wiped off recently. She opened it to find it was full of pictures, papers, magazines, and college textbooks. *Bernie's memorabilia from days gone by*, she thought.

As she rummaged through the contents of the trunk, she noticed a large amount of photos of women—some of them nudes. Some of the women were undressing and looked like they weren't aware anyone was photographing them. The photos were taken on a digital camera and printed on a photo printer. Since Marva didn't have a computer, Gen wondered where these pictures had come from. The college text books all had a medical theme—anatomy, kinesiology, the human mouth. *These must be Bernie's books*, she thought. *He probably stores his old materials in his mother's house. I'll ask Marva, tonight at supper, why someone was up in the attic on Sunday night for an hour.*

* * *

"This stew is delicious," Gen said, taking a second helping of the comfort food.

"Thanks," Marva beamed. "This is Oscar's recipe."

"Marva is a wonderful cook," Oscar said, smiling at Marva.

Marva blushed. "Oscar helps me lot. He's a pretty good cook too."

There was a moment of awkward silence. Gen changed the subject. "Tell me a little bit about Bernie," she said.

"Oh, we're all proud of Bernie," Marva said. "He worked very hard to get through college. I couldn't help him much with finances, so he had to have a job and government aid. Oscar helped him with the math and science when he was in high school and also college. I don't think he would have made it without Oscar's help."

"Oh, I didn't do much," Oscar said modestly.

"Is Bernie married?" Gen asked.

"Well, no." Marva hesitated. She didn't seem to want to pursue the subject of marriage or women any further.

"Bernie has lots of girlfriends," Benny popped into the conversation proudly. "He shows me pictures of them all the time." He giggled.

"Well, I-I'm not sure they are all his girlfriends," Marva stammered. "Just casual friends and women he works with."

"Bernie was home before Easter," Benny said. "He brought me a present."

"What did he bring you, Benny?" Gen asked.

"A digital camera. I can't use it much because we don't have a computer to put the picture on, but we could go into the photo shop in Bemidji and have them developed. Mom doesn't have time to go to Bemidji. I've been taking pictures."

"What type of pictures do you take?" Gen asked.

"I like birds and other animals. I also like flowers and pretty scenery. It will be really pretty outside soon. I'll take more pictures," Benny said.

"That's nice. I'd love to see some of your pictures sometime. I'll bet they are really good," Gen said.

"Bernie also brought home a big trunk we had to haul up into the attic. It was heavy. I helped," Benny said proudly.

Marva gave Benny a stern look. "Eat your stew, Benny. Remember, we're playing pinochle tonight."

Benny picked up his spoon and begin gobbling down his stew. Between large mouthfuls of stew, he smiled and said enthusiastically, "I like pinochle."

That trunk in the attic is Bernie's, Gen thought. *I wonder why he brought it home.*

* * *

Benny wanted to play with Gen, so Marva and Oscar were partners. Benny was not a bad pinochle player. At times he was a bit impulsive, but for the most part he played a good game. Gen marveled at his ability to focus and count the cards so he knew how to play a hand when he had the bid. He also beamed and was very proud of himself when he made a bid and when he and Gen won a game.

After three games, Gen and Benny had won two. Oscar announced that he had some work to do and went upstairs to his room.

Marva, Benny, and Gen continued playing three-handed pinochle. Benny was very lucky and got excellent cards, so he won all three games. He was very happy and didn't want to quit.

"We've got to let Gen get some sleep," Marva said to Benny. "We'll play again some other night."

Benny looked disappointed but got up from the table, put the cards away, and went to his room.

"He loves to play cards and games," Marva said. She paused for a moment, looking sad. "He also loves his brother and worships everything Bernie does." Marva paused again and then rambled on. "Too bad we can't afford a computer. We had one once, but it broke down and became outdated, so I couldn't get it fixed. I can't afford to replace it. I can live very nicely without a computer, but Benny would like one. He loves taking pictures and is pretty good at it—I think. He's trying to earn enough money by doing odd jobs around town to get a computer, but this is a small town, and people do most of their own small jobs."

Marva stopped talking and sat quietly in a melancholy mood.

Gen smiled. "He'll do okay; he looks determined." She got up from the table. "I'm going to bed," she announced. "I have to call my husband; then I'm crashing."

* * *

"That's strange," Fletch said when Gen gave him an abridged version of what she'd found in the attic. "He probably has a fetish for women's pictures—especially those that don't know they're being photographed."

"Another funny thing: he was home before Easter, and that was when Evie disappeared. Quite a coincidence," Gen said.

"Yeah, you're right. Maybe Bernie is some kind of a stalker—or worse, a serial killer."

"I think you're getting carried away here," Gen said. "I haven't heard anything about him even meeting Evie or being interested in her. I'll quiz Benny some more. He likes to talk about his smart brother. It seems like Bernie can manipulate Benny. Maybe he talked Benny into doing something foolish. Benny liked Evie. He's told me that many times."

"Let's hope that didn't happen. It would be really sad if the smart brother talked his less-intelligent brother into committing a crime—really sadistic!"

"Well, let's not jump to conclusions. Benny seems pretty innocent. I don't see him killing anyone."

"I'll do some investigating into Bernie's life," Fletch volunteered. "The bank has all kinds of ways to investigate people. We're always checking out backgrounds when it comes to loans. I'll see what I can find out about Bernie Jacobs."

"Good, that might help."

"In the meantime, if Bernie comes home, I want to know. I'm not sure you're safe in that house if he's around. After I do my investigation, we'll decide if you should stay there."

"Don't panic, Fletch," Gen scolded. "This may be just some young man's fantasy world we're looking at. Besides, I only have five more weeks to go. This first week has been very interesting. My first real teaching job, meeting a whole bunch of new people, and trying to solve a mystery. What could be more exciting? I'm looking forward to next week."

"I'm happy you're enthused about your job, but I don't want my girl hurt. Please be careful. The town of Little Beaver may be housing a murderer."

CHAPTER 10

Gentlemen, you can't fight in here! This is the War Room.
—*Dr. Strangelove* (1964)

Miracle of miracles! The two senior holdouts turned in their paragraph assignments on the most important things you've learned from your senior English assignments this year.

"Thank you all for getting your assignments in on time today," Gen said. "I'm excited to read what you have to say. Your last five weeks of senior English will be based on what you've written."

A few seniors smiled; the rest sat silently. The two holdouts, Danny Crow and Allen Agindos, were smirking in the back of the room. *I can't wait to read their paragraphs*, Gen thought.

During lunch Gen met the speech therapist, Miss Patricia Wanot. She was fiftyish, tall, thin, and had a very professional look about her. Her dark eyes reflected intelligence, and her salt-and-pepper hair was beautifully groomed.

After some friendly small talk, Gen asked, "Do you work with Dawn Kingfish?"

"Yes, I do," Pat answered.

"What can you tell me about her?"

"She stutters at times. Her biggest problem is not her speech or stuttering; it's her self-confidence. The girl comes from a dysfunctional home, to say the least. Heaven knows what goes on there. She doesn't like to talk about it. Maybe the counselor would know more about that than I do. I think when Dawn goes to college—where I think she'll do very well with all her athletic and academic skills—her stuttering problem will be under control."

Gen breathed a sigh of relief and said, "I'm very happy to hear that. She's such a nice girl."

Gen went back to her classroom with a smile on her face and a bounce in her step.

When Millie appeared in the doorway at 3:30, Gen was ready for her.

"Want to go for a Friday cocktail and supper?" Millie asked. "We can play poker afterward."

"I can't go after school. I told Marva I'd be home early for supper. Marva, Oscar, and Benny are going to a movie in Grand Falls tonight, so they want to eat about 5:00. I'll be over for poker later on. That sounds like fun. What time should I be there?"

"About 6:45. Poker starts at seven, but you need to sign in ahead of time."

"Okay, see you at 6:45."

* * *

The Coffee and Beer Café was humming when Gen arrived at 6:45. Millie was waiting for her at the bar. The six men from the elders' coffee group were there, along with Swen Swenson, D.J., Mary Gustafson, an elementary teacher, and her husband Gust, Benny, Liz Larson, a young Chippewa woman, three men Gen didn't know, and Ed, the café manager, who was running the poker game.

After signing in, Millie introduced Gen to the young Chippewa woman. "This is Rachel Elk; she works at the bank."

"Hi, Rachel. Played poker long?"

Rachel shrugged. "A few years," she answered.

Gen smiled, and Rachel smiled back. Neither lady seemed to think of anything else to say, so each drew a card that indicated where they should sit at table one or two.

Ed had set up two tables with nine players at each table. Gen and Millie were at table one, seats two and six. Elroy was the dealer at table one. Rachel was the dealer at table two.

Two of the unknown men were at table one. Millie introduced them. "Gen, this is Anton 'Tony' Crow and Delbert 'Bert' Charbonneau. These two rednecks are truckers. Don't pay too much attention to what they say; they both have potty mouths."

Millie snorted a laugh. Gen, Tony, and Bert joined her.

"Millie can hold her own with any trucker," Tony said.

Bert raised his eyebrows and nodded in agreement with Tony's statement. Millie shrugged.

The two truckers got up and went to the bar to get a drink. While they were gone, Millie told Gen about Tony and Bert's trucking jobs. "Tony delivers fuel to the convenience store every two weeks on Friday. He usually sleeps overnight in his big truck and leaves Saturday morning for Minneapolis, his home base. Bert delivers bread and other staple groceries to the convenience store every Tuesday or Friday. He plays poker when there's a game and stays overnight with the widow Olson.

"Bert claims the widow is his aunt, but he seems to have an aunt in every town where he stays overnight, so I don't know if he's telling the truth—but then, who cares." Millie laughed.

The truckers returned with their beers and sat down in their places.

"Sit down and be quiet! Let's start," Elroy said in a grumpy, authoritative tone, addressing those who were still milling around and visiting.

After everyone was seated, Ed told the group about the prize hands for the night. "The first player out wins a drink, 'Bubble Boy' wins a six-pack of beer, and the first player to win a hand on the river with a pair of pocket tens wins a drink. You can start."

Elroy dealt to see who would get the dealer button and who would be the small blind and the big blind. Once that was determined, the game was on.

Gen mucked her hands until she was the big blind. She was getting very poor hands to bet on. She checked on a queen of hearts and an eight of hearts, hoping to get three more hearts or a queen or eight on the flop. Millie and Tony called. The small blind folded. The flop produced a nine of hearts, a jack of clubs, and a three of spades. Gen now had three hearts for a flush and the possibility of an inside straight. Gen bet a hundred-dollar chip. Millie and Tony called. The turn produced a four of hearts. Gen now had four hearts for a flush. She bet two hundred-dollar chips. Millie and Tony called. *What could they have?* Gen thought.

An eight of diamonds came up on the river. Gen now had a pair of eights with a queen kicker. She bet two more hundred-dollar chips. Millie folded, and Tony called. Both players showed their hands. Tony had a pair of nines with a king kicker. He won.

The whole evening produced a series of losing hands for Gen. At one point she looked over at table two to see how they were doing and saw D.J. staring at her. She turned quickly. *Why is he staring at me?* she thought. *Maybe we're both bored at losing all the time.* Later, when she looked over at table two again, D.J. was gone.

The language got rougher, and tempers flared as the evening went on because people lost hands to players who were lucking out on inferior hands. The F word and the S word became more and more prominent. At one point Bert called Tony a moron for betting a large amount of money on pocket twos. Many thought that vulgarity was a form of wit, so the more they drank, the more vulgar they became.

Tony was a nervous twit who played with his chips and dropped them on top of each other constantly. Tony swore at Bert and told him to play his own hands and not to worry about other people's.

All the chip dropping and potty mouths drove Gen nuts. Bert was a bit more laid back than Tony. He smiled a lot because he was winning. This drove Tony crazy. The two were always arguing. At one point Tony got up and walked away from the table to calm himself down. He seemed to have a big anger-management problem.

"Geez, Tony," Doc said in his usual cantankerous tone of voice, "it's just a game of free poker."

Tony kept pacing and looking around like he was looking for someone. Then he asked of no one in particular, "Where's Evie?" He'd been on a delivery run down south and hadn't been in to play poker for a couple of weeks.

The table got quiet. "Didn't you know she was missing?" Doc asked. "They haven't found her yet, dead or alive."

"Oh," Tony said, shrugging his shoulders and looking perplexed. He was on his third beer, so his powers of deduction were limited.

"I've been gone for two weeks, dontcha know," Tony said. Then he dropped the subject like he didn't care one way or another.

Bert chuckled and said, "Evie sure was a girl that could curse with the best of them. I never could figure her out. She was well educated, smart, pretty in a way, but sure seemed to be an airhead."

"I think she lacked self-esteem," Doc said.

"BS," Tony said in a booming voice. "She had plenty of self-esteem. Were any of you ever out with her?"

The table got eerily quiet. Elroy looked down at his beer.

"Oh, shut up, Tony," Elroy said. "What do you know about self-esteem, you moron?"

The game continued. Liz went all in on a hand of pocket kings. Doc ended up with a flush, king high, so he beat Liz's king trips. Liz went home.

The second player out was Herman, who had been playing very conservatively but just wasn't hitting. Millie was next to leave the table.

Gen held her own by playing tightly and conservatively. When the break came, she had very few chips left, so she decided to make a big all-in move after the break. She'd either win some more chips or go home.

After the break, the players left in the game were all at one table. The first one out was Tony, and then Swen bit the dust. Gen went all in on the third hand played. She had a pair of pocket tens. Since that was the hand that could win a free drink, she decided to go for it. She was beat out by Bert, who had a pair of pocket jacks. *No free drink tonight.*

Gen joined Millie at the table of losers, who were having a beverage of choice before they went home.

"All done?" Millie asked when Gen sat down and ordered some coffee.

"Yes," Gen answered. "Doc and Bert seem to be doing the best. I guess they'll be the winners tonight."

"Yah." Millie nodded. "They're both good players."

"I think we should head for home," Mary Gustafson said to Gust. "We're getting company tomorrow, and I've got to do some cooking."

"Yah sure, you betcha," Swen chimed in with his thick Scandinavian brogue. "That's a good idea, Mary. I think we all need some sleep."

"Did you know Evie had a potty mouth?" Gen asked Millie after everyone else was gone from their table.

"She did here at the bar, after a few drinks. She was okay at school," Millie answered.

"I never heard her swear in college. I wonder what changed."

"She probably didn't have any reason to swear in college. She had plenty of reasons to be aggressive here. Lots of aggressive men with foul mouths here. I guess she wasn't going to let any of them get the best of her," Millie speculated.

"If she disliked them, why did she go out with so many of them?"

Millie smiled. "I don't know. I'm no psychologist, but my guess would be that she was looking for a father. I heard her say once that her father left home when she was very young. Girls like that often spend their whole life looking for the father they never had."

"You could be right," Gen agreed. "From what I know of human behavior, girls who are overly aggressive and in-your-face to men could have been sexually abused when they were kids. Do you think Evie was sexually abused?"

"How should I know? She didn't tell me much of her past. All I know is that she didn't like her stepfather—called him a real prick. She also called her mother a doormat."

"What do you mean, doormat?"

"Well, she let the men in her life walk all over her," Millie said.

"Oh!" Gen pondered a moment. "Maybe Evie's mother was a battered wife. Some women have so little self-esteem that they let their husbands beat them and think it's their fault."

"Pretty sick, isn't it?" Millie said and changed the subject. "What are you doing tomorrow?"

"Correcting papers. I can't wait to see what my seniors wrote in their paragraphs. I might also go for a walk. The countryside is really greening up. This area sure has a lot of beautiful scenery. I'll take my camera. Want to come along?"

"No, I'm going to Bemidji to shop. I need to spend some of that big paycheck we get." Millie snorted a laugh.

CHAPTER 11

Well, here's another nice mess you've gotten me into.
—*Sons of the Desert* (1933)

"Oh my God!" Gen exclaimed as she read her senior English class paragraphs on Saturday morning. She was reading the paper handed in by Allen Agindos. *The most important thing I learned my senior year was new sexual techniques from my senior English teacher, Miss Pretsler. She was something else!*

Allen went on to describe what Evie had taught him in great detail—obviously meant to shock Gen. He had succeeded in his efforts. He ended his assignment by writing, *All the hands-on stuff I learned from Miss Pretsler will serve me better in my life time than all that grammar crap you're trying to teach.*

Danny Crow's paper had similar material that included Miss Pretsler's working with him and Allen at the same time. "Terrible!" Gen gasped as she read the paragraphs Danny had written. *I'll have to decide what to do with this information. I'll talk to Fletch tonight, Millie tomorrow. They will probably have a better idea of what the proper procedure would be.*

After finishing the other ten senior papers and making appropriate comments on each paper, Gen decided to have some breakfast.

Marva, Benny, and Oscar were gone by the time she got downstairs to the kitchen. She'd missed breakfast.

Gen found a note on the kitchen counter: "Help yourself to anything you'd like to eat from the fridge. Benny and I will be gone for the day, shopping in Bemidji, while Oscar works with the Academic Pursuit Team. Have a nice day, Marva."

Gen had a microwaved egg and some wheat toast. As she ate, she worried about the two disturbing senior papers. *I need to get out of here, get some fresh air, clear my head; way too much school stress this past week!*

She finished eating her egg and toast and went upstairs, put on some walking shoes and a light jean jacket, grabbed her camera, and left the house. She'd heard there was a beautiful walking path north of town. She'd also heard about wild animals in the woods and knew she had to be careful.

About a half mile north of Little Beaver, along the lakeshore, she found a path made by animals that came down to the lake to drink. This path looked like it followed the edge of the lake around the west side. *If I stay close to the lake, I shouldn't get lost,* she thought.

Gen stopped at times to take pictures of what she thought was amazingly beautiful scenery: a loon swimming along the shore, a cluster of cattails nestled in a small cove, a group of pelicans swimming peacefully along the edge of the lake. *Fletch will love these pictures,* she thought. *He likes wildlife as much as I do.*

Gen entered a small clearing that had a sandy beach near the lake. She saw a young doe drinking on the shore.

She gasped, "Awesome!" She focused her camera, but the young doe saw her and bolted into the woods before she could take the picture.

"Shucks," she said out loud. Then she did a foolish thing: she followed the doe into the woods.

Fifteen minutes later she was hopelessly lost. *Why didn't I bring my cell phone? Why didn't I pay more attention to my Girl Scout leader back home when the woman tried to teach survival skills in the woods? What direction is south? Where is the sun? No north star to find. God, I hope I'm not still lost when the stars come out.* "Think, Gen, think!" she said to herself.

Gen trekked around in the woods. She walked beneath the jack pines, white spruce, box elders, and green ash, feeling like the forest had swallowed her whole. She passed through a stand of balsam firs that looked familiar. *Have I been here before?*

She finally decided to mark a spot in the trail with a facial tissue she had in her pocket. Ten minutes later she found the tissue where she had left it. *I'm going around in circles*, she realized. She sat down on the ground to clear her head and make a plan.

"Stay calm! Crying won't help," she said to herself. "You've got to go in one direction. Find the sun. Stay focused on it." Her watch read four o'clock. *You've got about two hours of sunlight left*, she assured herself.

She followed the sun, which was starting to go down in the west. There were times the trees were so thick, she couldn't see the sun, but there were also times when there were clearings in the forest and she could get refocused.

After an hour of trekking west, she stumbled onto a gravel road—not a very good road but a road nonetheless. She was delirious with joy. The road ran north and south, if her reckoning was correct. *Which way should I go?* As she debated, she noticed some smoke above the tree line to the north. *Maybe someone lives in a cabin over there? They wouldn't build a gravel road to nowhere!*

Gen walked a little faster and came to a clearing with wood fences, where the trees had been removed and only stumps remained. Her heart started to hammer from the exercise and excitement. There were cattle and horses grazing peacefully in the pasture. At the end of the pasture was a log cabin and a long, low barn or shed. *Somebody lives here!*

She crossed a bridge that traversed a stream in front of the cabin. Quickening her steps, she was soon standing on the front porch of the cabin, knocking on the door.

Gen heard a dog bark. It sounded like a big dog.

Oh, God. All I need now is to tangle with a big dog!

She heard a man's voice. The dog stopped barking. The door opened. Her heartbeat was racing.

"Well, I'll be darned!" D.J. said in a surprised tone. He was holding the big dog by the collar.

Gen gasped. She couldn't speak for a second. Then she stammered, "S-so sorry to disturb you. I-I'm ..."

"Lost?" he finished her sentence.

"Well, yes. I-I was ..."

"Out walking and followed a deer into the woods and couldn't find your way out?" he asked.

"Well, yes, but—" She stopped talking because she didn't know how to explain her stupidity.

He smiled. "Don't worry. It happens a lot. You city folks don't realize how dangerous it can be in a thick forest when you can't see anything but trees."

He was being a male chauvinist again, but Gen wasn't going to challenge him. He was in the catbird seat.

"I'm sorry." She hung her head. "I-I ..."

"Don't be sorry," he interrupted. "I like company. Come on in."

She hesitated. "Well, I really need to get home and—" She paused. Her heart was pumping.

He looked at her and shook his head in disgust. "Do you know the way home?"

"Well, no, but ..."

"If you want me to drive you, you'll have to wait until I've eaten my supper. It's all ready, and I've got plenty for you, too. You're probably starved after that long walk in the woods."

She looked around the room. The wooden logs showed on the walls—very rustic looking. The room was about sixteen by twenty feet with a small kitchen at the east end. The wooden floors were beautifully finished and clean. There were two doors leading off the west side of the room—bath and bedroom, she assumed.

The aroma coming from the kitchen made Gen's mouth water. She hadn't eaten since this morning, when she had the egg and toast.

"It smells very good, but I don't want to impose. I-I …"

He cut her off midsentence and said in a soft, inviting voice, "Come on in. I won't bite." He smiled and cocked his head to the side in an innocent, puppylike fashion.

Gen smiled back and took a deep breath. She entered the cabin and stood frozen on the doormat. She wasn't sure she should go any further with D.J., and she sure didn't want to disturb the big dog at his side, who was keeping an eye on her.

"For God's sake," he said, "what has Millie been telling you about me? I'm not some kind of monster. I don't attack women—geez!"

"Well, I-I …"

"Come on, sit down. I'll serve you some of my world-famous stew."

Gen looked at the dog and remained frozen on the doormat. The dog was about two and a half feet high and weighed about eighty pounds. He was white with black around his eyes and ears and black splotches on his body. His snout was white. He looked like some breed of hunting dog.

D.J. laughed. "This is Hunter. He wouldn't hurt a flea, would you, boy?" He reached over and scratched Hunter between the ears. "Go lay down," D.J. commanded the dog.

Hunter obeyed and lay down near the stone fireplace, which was surrounded by a tile hearth.

D.J. took Gen's hand and led her to the table.

Gen followed him robotically, walking stiff-legged and keeping one eye on the dog. Then she wondered, *Should I be watching the dog or D.J.?*

She sat down when he pulled a chair out for her. He patted her on the back. "Relax, I've never killed anyone with my stew!" He laughed.

Gen smiled and laughed with him, trying to appear calm. *How did he know that I was just wondering if he killed Evie after feeding her his world-famous stew?*

CHAPTER 12

Of all the gin joints in all the towns in all
the world, she walks into mine.
—*Casablanca* (1942)

D.J. brought her a steaming bowl of delicious-smelling stew along with a soup spoon and butter knife. He put a plate full of sliced homemade bread and some butter on the table. Then he filled another bowl with stew and brought it over to the table and sat down.

Gen watched him intently. She noticed how easily he moved about his small kitchen and how comfortable he was in his own surroundings.

"Okay, let's eat!" he said with a smile.

Gen picked up her spoon, filled it with stew, blew on it to cool it, and took a little sip. "Still hot," she said as she laid down her spoon, "but it's delicious."

"Deer stew," he said.

"Yes, I know," Gen said with a smile. "My dad was a hunter, and we ate lots of wild game while we were growing up."

"Where'd you live?" he asked.

"On a small, diversified farm in southwestern Minnesota. Near Fairmont. Do you know where that is?"

"I've never been there, but I know it's along Interstate 90."

"Correct." She was impressed.

He smiled. "You're not the only one with a college degree. I have a BA from the University of Minnesota, with majors in human science and business administration."

"Human science?" Gen's eyebrows went up as she studied him closely.

"Yes. I thought I wanted to work with people, but after the war, I changed my mind."

"In what way?"

He thought for a moment, weighing his response. "Wars are hell—whether you win or lose. The United States doesn't seem to win wars anymore. They just go into countries and kill people, destroy their property, and then eventually leave. We say it's for the good of those people, but what we're really doing is taking care of our world economy and all the greedy large businesses overseas. There are very few people left that think more of other people's welfare than their own."

"I can't disagree with you on that, but we can't let the terrorists come over here and destroy us."

"Okay, then let's protect our borders and take care of our own people and leave other people alone," he suggested.

"That's the way it should be, but the religious fanatics want to destroy our way of life and our religion. They think their way is the only way," she rebutted.

"Yes, that's true, but then many of our people think that our religion and way of life is the only way too. It works both ways."

"You're right, but I just trust us a little more than I do them."

He chuckled while stroking his beard. "Religion and politics are two subjects you should never discuss over a meal; it can ruin your appetite. Let's change the subject. What was it like growing up on a small, diversified farm in southwestern Minnesota?"

Gen smiled. "It was great. I was the second of four children— an older sister and two younger brothers. Our parents were always home, being farmers. Mom helped Dad, and we had a lot of family chores and togetherness. We raised turkeys and pigs. What a combination, huh?"

"Sounds fine to me," he said. "I raise horses, Indian ponies, and purebred hunting dogs—German shorthair pointers. I train both. I also have a few cattle and chickens—need eggs and meat to eat, dontcha know."

Gen nodded. "Tell me about the Indian ponies. Are they a pure breed of horse or what?"

"The American Indian pony is known by many other names— Spanish pony, cow pony, mustang, Cayuse, and buffalo horse. Very few of them have a pure bloodline anymore. They have no specific features to identify their breed. Their features vary according to the horses that were crossbred with them. The American Indian captured the wild ones and bred them for riding and hunting. Did you know the Spanish explorers first brought the breed to this country?"

Gen nodded. "What do most of yours look like?"

"They are white with black splotches. They're about fifteen hands high and are used mostly as show horses and for riding."

"Do you exhibit them?" she asked.

"Yes, I've been showing my horses since I was twelve in 4H exhibits and county and state fairs. They've won some prizes."

"Congratulations." She paused. "Who do you sell them to?"

"Mostly to people who want a smaller riding horse. There used to be two million of these ponies running around wild in the western United States; now we're down to about thirty thousand. I'm trying to keep the breed alive. I think they are a terrific horse with lots of character and resilience."

Gen smiled. *This guy has lots of character himself, and he certainly seems to be self-sufficient.*

There was a moment of silence as each sat mulling over his or her own thoughts and observations. D.J. broke the silence. "Have you ever ridden a horse?"

Gen laughed. "Duh! Living on a farm—what do you think?"

He smiled. "Well, maybe you weren't into horses. Not everyone that grows up on a farm likes horses."

"True, but I'm not one of those people. I love horses. We had a little mare named Silver, who was half Arabian and half something else. She was so gentle with us kids. We all learned to ride on her. I did some competitive barrel racing in high school, and I also worked at training horses for barrel racing during my 4H days. You're not the only one who has some 4H ribbons," she teased.

There was another moment of silence as they ate their stew. They both seemed to be comfortable to sit and reflect on what had been said.

Gen broke the silence. "How about the dogs? The German shorthair pointers? Is Hunter one of them?" she asked.

"Yes, he's my favorite—great hunting dog and a good pet. Hunter has sired my puppies. I have two female dogs, Gretchen and Heidi. They're kept in the shed. They'll both have puppies soon."

"So the male gets to live in the warm house and the females and children get to live in the cold shed?" Gen asked in mock frustration.

"It's not like that," he said defensively. "The shed is modern, clean, warm, and just right for raising puppies in."

"Sorry," Gen said. "I didn't mean to imply that you didn't take care of the females and puppies. I guess I misspoke." *I don't want to upset this guy,* she thought.

"That's okay." He flashed a smile. "I'll take you out there and show you when the puppies are born. You'll love them; they're so much fun. I love it when they're old enough to take outside. Their energy just cracks me up."

"We had dogs and puppies on our farm, but none were purebred, so we gave them away," Gen recalled in a whimsical tone. "Dad usually ended up having our females spayed because he didn't want a whole bunch of dogs around, but we kids sure had fun with them when they were puppies."

Another moment of silence ensued as they smiled at each other, talking of their days as kids with a bunch of puppies around.

"So what do your puppies look like? Will they all look like Hunter?" Gen asked, anxious to continue the convivial atmosphere.

"Most will, but there's sometimes a throwback that looks like some relative in the past. I get an occasional dark-brown-and-white puppy or a slightly different shade of black puppy with different types of markings."

"What do people buy your dogs for?" Gen asked.

"Mostly hunting, but they also make great pets, and they're friendly. They reflect a nice balance of performance and personality. They retrieve on land and in water and have keen noses if you're looking for a good hunting dog. But they're not perfect!" D.J. laughed like he was hiding a secret.

"What's wrong with them?" Gen wanted to know.

"They can be hyper, and they sure eat a lot. Now Hunter over there is really laid back. That's why I raised him as a sire—hoping most of the puppies would be calm like he is. But even with that fault, I wish I could put them on hold before they're old enough to sell, so I could keep them longer."

He paused a moment and then continued enthusiastically. "They need a lot of exercise too. I'm really glad I live out here where I can turn them loose and they can run and play freely. I couldn't do that in town."

There was another moment of silence as they both finished their meal.

"You must like black and white," Gen broke the silence. "Your horses are black and white, your dogs are black and white, and I noticed when I came here that your cattle are black. Must be Angus?"

"Yes, good beef cattle. I also have a milk cow. I call her Matilda. She's a milking mixed breed—Angus are not milkers. I get plenty of milk from Matilda, and what I don't use, I feed to the dogs; they love it."

"I'll bet they do!" Gen chuckled with a mischievous look in her eye. "You certainly are self-sufficient. I suppose you even raise a garden?"

"Yup. I'll be planting my potatoes soon, as soon as the ground warms up."

There was another moment of silence. D.J. looked at Gen intently, which gave her a feeling of warmth.

"I really should be going," Gen murmured, feeling very uncomfortable. "Can I help you with the dishes?"

"No, Hunter does that!" he joked.

"Clever dog."

She sat silently thinking about the gossip that would ensue in Little Beaver if she got home too late and was dropped off by that old, red pickup. "I'd better be going," she said.

"Just relax a moment," he begged. "I'm enjoying our conversation. I don't often get to talk to an attractive, intelligent woman."

She said nothing, momentarily daunted. *What will Fletch think? What will Millie say? What will my students write next?*

D.J. seemed to read her mind. "How long have you been married?" he asked out of the blue.

"Two years!" she answered curtly. *Why is that any of his business?*

"I was married for three years before I was sent to Iraq."

"Oh?" Gen said, trying to sound surprised, although she knew all about D.J.'s wife and didn't care a bit about his marriage.

"Michelle was a city girl—beautiful, smart, but totally self-centered. I loved her and was so smitten by her, I didn't notice the self-centered part until we moved out here. As long as we lived in Minneapolis, where she could do her things with her family and friends, everything was hunky-dory. She loved going to parties and showing off the good-looking hunk of man she had married. She never did care much about what I wanted. After I got my orders to go to Iraq, I brought her home to stay with my mother until I got back."

Gen nodded while trying to fake an interest in his past marriage.

"Michelle was miserable out here. She couldn't find a thing to do without her restaurants, theaters, musicals, shopping sprees, and fake friends. So while I was in Iraq, she went back to the city and started running around with her old friends again. When I got home, I had divorce papers waiting."

"Sorry to hear that. Maybe the two of you should never have gotten married, being from such different backgrounds."

"You got that right!" he said bitterly. Then he took a deep breath to calm himself.

He paused a moment and then said in a melancholy tone of voice, "I doubt I'll ever find a girl who wants to live out here in the woods with me and raise horses, dogs, and kids."

"Oh, I don't know." Gen paused. She was starting to feel sorry for him; he was getting to her. "There are lots of nice girls who might want to be here. Maybe you need to be a little more flexible in your thinking."

He stared at her for a moment and then changed the subject. "What's your real name? It can't be Gen!"

"It's Genevieve. I hate it—too long and girlish."

"Genevieve," he said softly. Then he said "Genevieve" again in an affectionate, longing tone. "I like it."

She looked into his beautiful brown eyes, and she didn't like what she saw. She was getting too warm, too relaxed, too emotional, too flustered. All she could think to say was, "I hear you write poetry?" *Where in the world did that come from?* she thought after the words had slipped out of her mouth.

"Who told you that?" He acted surprised, wrinkling his brow.

She thought a moment. "Charlie McCann did."

"Good old Charlie!" He flashed one of his sexy smiles. "Well, I kind of write poetry. Want to hear some?"

"Well, I guess. Maybe one poem. Your favorite. I really have to go."

He left the room and went through a side door that led to his bedroom. She turned her head and looked at the fireplace and Hunter, who was sleeping soundly on the rug.

Lord, how am I going to get out of here? she thought as she walked over to the couch and sat down.

He returned shortly with a folder full of plastic holders containing sheets of paper, sat down on the couch next to her, and opened the folder.

Gen read the first poem. "Your style is a bit like Carl Sandburg— short, to the point, using common thoughts and language."

D.J. smiled. "I'm glad you noticed. Sandburg is my hero. He's my kind of poet."

"What's your favorite Sandburg poem?"

"'Chicago.'"

"Why?"

"Because he's telling the reader that some people may not have a lot of culture, but they work and put up with things so they can eat regularly. I think he admires those people from that cultural background."

"I agree." Gen smiled. "My favorite Sandburg poem is 'Fog.' It's short, to the point, and compares fog to the whimsical moment of a cat. I like the imagery. The cat is silent and skillful— so is the fog."

D.J. smiled. He turned the folder to the last page, where Carl Sandburg's "At a Window" was printed out. He had copied it off the internet and underlined some of the lines, which he read:

Give me hunger, pain and want …
But leave me a little love,
A voice to speak to me at the days end,
A hand to touch me in the dark room
Breaking the long loneliness …
And wait and know the coming
Of a little love.

When he finished reading, he said, "Do you suppose that will ever happen for me?"

Gen didn't answer but read out loud what he had written at the bottom of the Sandburg poem:

"Don't tell me about love,
When I'm with the things
I love but human love escapes me.
Someone to talk to,
To touch, to hold, to caress.
Someone to share the things I love with.
I search—where are you?"

When she finished reading, she looked into D.J.'s eyes and saw a hunger there that she could never fulfill.

"You'd better take me home. It's getting late," she whispered while lowering her eyes to where her hands were trembling.

CHAPTER 13

You talking to me?
—*Taxi Driver* (1976)

I t was only eight thirty when D.J. dropped Gen off at the Bumblebee Inn, but it seemed like a lifetime to her. No one spoke on the three-and-a-half-mile ride to town. The silence seemed to be called for.

"Thanks for supper and the lift," Gen mumbled as she quickly hopped out of the pickup after D.J. stopped in the driveway at the front of the inn.

"My pleasure," D.J. said softly, sporting a sexy grin.

Gen rushed into the house and slammed the door quickly, like some monster was after her. Her knees were shaking. She leaned against the door for support. Her breath came in short gasps, and her pulse raced as she tried to calm herself. He hadn't touched her, but he'd certainly gotten to her.

Gen walked to the kitchen after she'd composed herself, to make a cup of tea. She sat down at the counter to analyze her feelings. *Is it guilt? Is it fear? Is it apprehension? Is it affection? It's certainly not love! Good grief, girl, pull yourself together.*

She sipped her hot tea and tried to relax. She certainly couldn't call Fletch until she had calmed down. Marva, Benny, and Oscar would be home soon. She didn't want them to find her all flustered.

Fifteen minutes later, she was in her room, calling Fletch.

He answered on the second ring. "Where have you been? I've been worried sick about you!"

"Sorry, honey. Please don't be angry. I've got a lot to tell you. So much has happened today that my head is spinning." Gen took a deep breath.

Fletch's voice softened. "Okay, calm down. What happened today?"

Gen started the narrative by telling Fletch about the two senior boys' papers.

"You've got to tell someone in authority," he said firmly when she stopped for a breath. "If you don't, you'll be withholding evidence on a possible murder investigation."

"I know," Gen wailed. "I'll tell the school principal on Monday morning, even if it means I never teach again."

"Maybe you should call him tomorrow morning. Don't wait!"

"I don't even know if he's home this weekend. And anyway, I want to talk to Millie first and see what the proper school procedure is."

"Well, I guess you could always say you didn't read the papers until late Sunday night. That should cover your butt. These things need to be reported immediately," Fletch warned.

"I guess you're right. I just don't want to rush to any conclusions and get the principal mad at me. I'll have to get a good recommendation from him at the end of the year if I want to find another job next fall."

"Okay, I understand." Fletch took a deep breath. "You sure have fallen into a mess on your first job. Sorry I can't be of more help, sweetheart." He paused a moment. Then on a more upbeat note, he said, "Wait until you hear what I found out about Bernie, the dentist."

"More bad news?"

"Yes. It seems he's on leave right now from his dentistry practice with Lock, Lowe, and Jacobs. According to the information I've obtained, he's been accused by several patients of lurid and unbecoming behavior toward women patients. Bernie seems to have a thing for pretty women. He says and does suggestive things while fixing their teeth."

"Wow!" Gen took a deep breath. "I wonder if Marva knows. She's such a sweet lady. She already has one son who's mentally challenged. She doesn't need another one with sexual deviance problems."

There was a moment of silence while Fletch decided what to say next. "If Bernie ever comes home again, I want to know. If he's carried his sexual fantasies too far with Evie, I don't want you in that house with that pervert. Maybe you can stay with Millie while he's home or something. If it's just for a weekend, I'll come up and stay with you."

"Thanks, sweetheart. I appreciate your concern. I'll be careful. He probably won't do anything wrong around his mother."

"His mother can't watch him twenty-four/seven. Please let me know if he comes home?"

"Okay, I promise I'll let you know."

Gen paused and took a deep breath. *Here goes. I'll have to tell him about D.J. and getting lost.*

Gen relayed most of the story, leaving out all her feelings and the poetry session. *If Fletch finds out about the romantic poetry D.J. writes, he'll hit the roof.*

"Sells horses and hunting dogs?" Fletch asked when she was done with her story. "If I get up that way, I'll have to see those dogs. My friends and I could use a good hunting dog this fall."

"Sure, if you get up here, I'll call D.J. and see if we can look at his dogs."

Gen took a deep breath and relaxed. *Good, Fletch is only focused on the dogs—just like a man. I'll ignore D.J. for five more weeks, and then I'll forget him entirely for the rest of my life!*

After some more casual talk and romantic banter, they said their good nights. Gen breathed a big sigh of relief. She'd been as honest as possible with Fletch. *Some things are better left unsaid.*

* * *

Gen slept like a baby that night. The long walk in the woods, all the fresh air, and the calming phone call to Fletch drained her of all her anxiety. When she awoke on Sunday morning, she felt refreshed. She heard voices downstairs. *Good, someone is up. I'm starved.*

She put on her house robe and went downstairs, where Marva and Oscar were making breakfast. "Good morning," Gen chirped.

"My, someone is in a good mood this morning," Marva said with a smile.

"I slept very well after my long walk yesterday," Gen said.

"Oh?" Oscar raised an eyebrow. "Where'd you go?"

Gen relayed the whole adventure to Marva and Oscar, leaving out feelings and poetry again.

"So you've had an encounter with our local Romeo?" Oscar grinned while giving Gen a suspicious look. "You seem to have recovered from his charms very nicely."

Gen blushed, giving Oscar a *please don't question me* look.

Oscar got the message and changed the subject. "Want to go to church with us? Starts in an hour."

"Sure." Gen smiled. "A little praying wouldn't hurt. It might help me make it through next week's school sessions."

Everyone laughed.

After church Marva served delicious homemade chicken noodle soup with big slices of homemade bread. Gen had three helpings. The meal reminded her of her mother's home cooking.

The conversation at lunchtime centered around the trio's trip to Bemidji on Saturday. Marva talked about the spring outfit she'd purchased at Penney's, Oscar talked about the new fishing equipment he'd purchased for the summer, and Benny chatted endlessly about the things he'd seen and done.

"We were in the new Wal-Mart," Benny said. "They have lots of stuff. I got my pictures developed there. Want to see them, Mrs. Fletcher?"

"Sure, I'd love to, Benny. After lunch, okay?"

"Okay," Benny answered cheerfully.

When all had eaten their fill, Marva said, "Oscar and I will clear the table, and Benny can show Gen his pictures."

Benny rushed into the living room and got his envelopes full of pictures out of the antique chest of drawers. He sat down on the old couch and beckoned for Gen to join him.

Gen looked at each picture carefully as Benny explained where and how he'd taken it. She smiled, oohed, aahed, and made a variety of positive comments as they reviewed the photos. The pictures were of scenery, animals, birds, and close-ups of flowers, shrubs, and trees.

"These are very good, Benny," Gen said when they were done. "You have a good eye for photography. I love the light you catch on these photos and also the types of subjects you choose to capture. Your color, distance, and focus are excellent."

Benny beamed. "Bernie taught me how to do all this. I just do what he tells me."

I hope he hasn't taught you to do anything wrong, Gen thought. "Why don't you frame some of these and try to sell them? People might buy them for gifts, dontcha know."

"I hadn't thought about that."

Marva put down her crocheting and jumped into the conversation. "Benny does nice woodwork too. He's made me some picture frames in the past, and I'm sure he'd get better at it if he practiced."

"You might use the money you make to buy a computer," Oscar suggested, looking up from the Sunday paper he was reading.

Benny got excited, beaming from ear to ear. "I've got lots of old lumber out in the shed in back of the house. I could use some of that."

"Yes, you could," Marva agreed.

"I'll be your first customer," Gen said. "Let me see those pictures again."

Benny handed the pictures to Gen as he jumped up off the couch and ran to the back door. Gen picked out three beautiful pictures of animals: a squirrel scampering across a colorful leaf-laden path in the woods, a fox peeking out from behind a small rock surrounded by flowering bushes, and a young fawn standing knee deep in wildflowers and looking very surprised and confused.

Benny came back into the living room carrying some wood samples. Gen chose an unpainted, aged barn wood.

"Can you make these three photos with the same frames, so I can hang them as a group?" she asked.

"I'll try," he answered.

"Good. That's all I can ask for. I'll give them to my husband for his birthday at the end of next month."

Benny scurried off to the shed, eager to start his project right away.

Marva beamed with maternal pride. She was happy to see that Benny would be busy with something to do. "It's so nice of you to encourage him like that," she said to Gen. "He gets so restless at times, and I worry about him. This will keep him busy for a long time."

Gen smiled. "I meant every word I said about his photos. I really do think they're very good."

Marva's eyes began tearing up.

"Well," Oscar said, clearing his throat and getting up out of the recliner where he'd been reading, "I'm going for a walk. Want to come along, Marva?"

"Love to." Marva got up from her chair and went to fetch her jacket.

"I hope we don't get lost like Gen did," Oscar teased with a wink.

Gen shook her head and grinned. "I hope so too. I'm going to call Millie, to see if I can talk to her about something. Maybe we can go for a stroll by the lake."

* * *

The teaching duo was sitting on a dock that looked out across the peaceful lake at the edge of town. Gen broke the news about her two senior boys' writing assignments.

"What!" Millie exclaimed with horror, unable to believe what she was hearing. "I knew there was something wrong in Evie's senior classes. Some of the kids whispered about it in the halls. As soon as I got close enough to hear, they clammed up. This is not good for the kids, for Evie, or for the school!"

"Do you think I should tell Haugen or the sheriff?" Gen asked, dangling her feet in the water.

"We've got a policy somewhere in our school bylaws that says things like this that can affect the school in any negative way must be reported to the administration. You've got to tell Haugen or Superintendent Gray—but he's not always here, and I think you have to do this right away—Monday morning, first thing!" Millie warned.

"What do I say?" Gen asked.

"You don't have to say anything; just give him the papers and let him decide what to do. It's his job!"

"Should I make copies?"

"By all means. Make two copies. Give one back to the students with appropriate comments, give the original to Haugen, and you keep a copy in case the other two are destroyed. You need to cover your butt."

"That's what I'm afraid of. If I've read Haugen right, he doesn't want waves in his tranquil sea. He thinks he's doing a perfect job here."

"You're right about that," Millie agreed. "This is one of those situation where you're damned if you do and damned if you don't. You've just got to go with the truth and let the chips fall where they may."

Gen sighed, a worried look on her face. "I know you're right. Fletch said about the same thing. It's hard when I know the truth can get me involved in a big mess and probably affect my future teaching career."

"Yah," Millie said softly. "Tough break, kid."

The two friends sat in commiseration on the dock, dangling their bare feet into the cold water.

CHAPTER 14

I'm going to make him an offer he can't refuse.
—*The Godfather* (1972)

Haugen sat speechless, reading the papers Gen had given him. When he finished, he said, "Well, Mrs. Fletcher, this is certainly a fine kettle of fish you've gotten us into!"

"Excuse me?" Gen was shocked. "How is this my fault?"

"You shouldn't make such open-ended assignments. You should be more specific."

"How much more specific do I need to be than 'write a few short paragraphs about the most important things you've learned from your senior English assignments this year, and you can also make suggestions for lessons in this class during the remainder of this year'?" Then she added as an afterthought, "Besides, this was one of the assignments suggested in our grammar book!"

Haugen sat quietly, staring at Gen. "Well, you don't need to do everything suggested in the book!"

Gen didn't reply. She had to work with this man on the problem that confronted them. If she got on his bad side, he'd nail her on recommendations, and that would be the end of a promising teaching career.

After a few moments, he said. "You can go to your class now. I'll take care of this."

Gen left the office and went to her first-period English class. When the buzzer rang, the seniors filed in quietly and took their seats. They knew what was going on; Gen could sense it in their demeanor, which gave them away.

Gen handed back their Friday assignment papers. She had made comments on all the papers. Each of the two young men who had written the controversial papers got special comments: "The grammar usage on your paper is mostly correct. What is not correct I have changed in red ink. Your subject matter is totally inappropriate for school assignments. I will not now or ever give you a grade on such subject matter. Your original paper has been turned over to Principal Haugen, who will decide what to do with the material. Since you are obviously an intelligent young man, I do not want to give you a failing grade the last six weeks of your English class. Please do the assignment work I give in an appropriate way from now on. Mrs. Fletcher."

Gen had also made a list of suggestions given by students for future English assignments. She handed out the list and asked for discussion.

Number one on the list was to help students fill out forms for college entrance, ACT and SAT tests, scholarships, summer employment, and so on.

Number two was to help students create résumés for future use.

Number three was to take an interest test, because many students still didn't know what they wanted to do after high school.

Number four was to take a field trip that would fit into the English and literature curriculum.

Number five was to study for and take a final test on English grammar usage.

Many of the assignments could be done in pairs or in groups of three and four.

After the discussion, Gen said she'd write a syllabus to let students know what was required of them for the remainder of the year. She then gave them the assignment for Tuesday. Students were to bring some forms they needed to fill out. They could fill out the information they knew at home. They were to make a copy of the form, so they had something to practice on.

The buzzer sounded. All the students left except Allen and Danny, who came walking up to Gen's desk.

"You'll be sorry you told the principal about our papers!" Danny whispered, giving Gen a supercilious look.

"Yah!" Allen echoed, with dark, brooding eyes fixed on Gen.

She was not intimidated. "I'm sorry you wrote what you did. You made the choice to tell about your escapades with Miss Pretsler. Now you'll have to suffer the consequences," she said softly but firmly.

"What's wrong with telling the truth?" Danny snapped.

"Nothing. The problem lies with the activity that went on between you two and Miss Pretsler. It's not appropriate for teachers to participate in such activity with students. Miss Pretsler was doing wrong. However, now that she's disappeared, you two could be involved with a crime."

"If *she* did wrong, why pick on us?" Allen was in an argumentative mood.

"Unfortunately, you'll be involved in this investigation now, whether you like it or not. It could get messy. I'm not involved in this problem, so I don't know what will happen. I certainly hope you young men have learned a lesson. If something is inappropriate, don't get involved—period! It reflects on your character. These records can stay with you for a long time and may even be permanent, since you are both eighteen years old. However, this is not my problem. I only ask that you do not hand in any inappropriate assignments again."

Gen paused a moment. The boys stood stubbornly by her desk, glaring at her with smug distain in their dark eyes. They made no attempt to leave.

"You both need to be going to your next classes, or you'll be late."

With that said, Gen got out her history book and started preparing for her next class. She ignored the boys standing by her desk.

The pair reluctantly left the room with mutinous looks on their faces. *I wonder what they'll do next*, Gen thought.

* * *

"That's a real bummer!" Millie sympathized as she sipped her beer at the local watering hole after school. "That Haugen can be a real prick!"

Gen nodded. "I feel sorry for those two boys. They have been so misguided. Do you have any background on them?"

"Both live with single mothers who work and aren't always home at night. I'm afraid they get into lots of trouble without proper adult supervision," Millie said. "I just hope we find Evie soon—one way or another. This whole thing is getting out of hand."

Gen sighed. "I think I'll talk to Charlie and see how the investigation is coming." She got up from her chair and wandered over to the bar. "Hi, Charlie." Gen patted the old man on the back. "How are things going?"

"Good, Mrs. Fletcher, good." Charlie grinned.

"So tell me, what did they find on Evie's cell phone?"

"Not much. Just calls home and several calls to a guy named Joe who lives in Seattle, dontcha know."

"Maybe she's with Joe in Seattle?" Gen surmised.

"Maybe. I guess they've been looking for Joe but can't seem to find anyone with that name and phone number. The calls were made to and from a payphone near a homeless shelter. Maybe they used the name Joe to throw people off. It could be a decoy."

"If I know Evie and the people she likes to hang with, Joe is probably another homeless drug user. Evie was a strange girl," Gen said.

Charlie nodded and took a sip of his beer.

"Come to think of it," Gen continued, "what happened to her car?"

"She never had one, as far as anyone knows. Her parents brought her here in the fall and got her for vacations. Otherwise she was on her own. I'm not even sure she had a driver's license." Charlie shrugged and looked perplexed.

"Maybe she had one and lost it. She probably got a DUI or two and couldn't get a license anymore. She drank too much, even in college, and I've heard that didn't change much here."

Charlie shrugged and smiled.

Charlie doesn't have a car or drive either, Gen thought. *He's probably missing a driver's license too. I guess I'd better drop this subject.*

"Well, like I said, Charlie, if you hear anything, I'd like to know."

Gen waved to Ed to bring Charlie another beer. Then she made her way back to Millie's table, where Elroy and Graywolfe had joined the teacher.

"That's what Sheriff Schultz said." Elroy was talking about the missing-teacher case.

"What did the sheriff say?" Gen asked as she sat down with the threesome.

"The sheriff said that Hunter, D.J.'s dog, brought home a bone yesterday—a human bone. The dog had been chewing on it. D.J. took the bone to the sheriff to have it examined."

"It's probably an old bone from the old Native American burial grounds near D.J.'s farm," Graywolfe said. "Every once in a while, someone finds one of those bones someplace that's been dug up by some wild animal. They'll send it to Minneapolis and do some forensics on it to determine if it's old or new."

"I guess so," Elroy agreed. "I'll have to call the sheriff tomorrow to see what they found out."

With that, Elroy got up and left the bar as D.J. entered. Gen finished her beer quickly and got up to leave.

"Where are you going in such a hurry?" Millie asked. "It's only four thirty.

"I've got lots of schoolwork to do tonight—gotta rush."

Gen walked briskly past D.J., not making eye contact. He grabbed her arm and turned her around. "What's your hurry?" he said with a friendly smile.

"I-I've got lots to do—homework, you know?" She tried to free her arm.

He hung on. "Don't rush off yet. Have another drink. I'll buy."

"No, thanks. I've had one—my limit. Please let go of my arm."

"Okay, sorry. I didn't realize you were so busy." D.J. let go of her arm, and she scurried out the door.

"What's with her?" D.J. asked Millie as he sat down at her table.

"She saw you and made a beeline for the door. I guess you just affect some women that way. Excuse me. I need to see a friend about a favor."

Millie got up and left the table.

Graywolfe looked at D.J. and shrugged. "Women! Who can ever figure them out? I sure can't."

"Yah," D.J. said wistfully, "neither can I."

CHAPTER 15

I'm mad as hell, and I'm not going to take this anymore!
—*Network (1967)*

This had arguably been the most depressing three days of Gen's life. Haugen was ignoring her; Allen and Danny were sitting in the back of the room, pouting and giving her mutinous looks. She couldn't go to the bar for fear she'd run into D.J. And to top it all off, Fletch was at a Wells Fargo loan officers' conference in Dallas and had left his cell phone home, so she couldn't get hold of him.

Walking home from school on hump day, Gen felt like she was carrying the weight of the world on her shoulders. She went directly to the kitchen when she reached the Bumblebee Inn, hoping to find Marva there—a friendly face to talk to. Marva reminded Gen of her mother, always cooking and cleaning and easy to talk to. *Maybe I'm homesick*, she thought.

"Hi, sweetie," Marva said, looking up from the pie crust she was rolling out on the counter. "You look like you've just lost your best friend."

"That's exactly how I feel," Gen said. "Got a minute to talk?"

"Sure. I'll just keep making supper, and you tell me what's bothering you."

Gen couldn't talk about the senior boys' papers or her feelings for D.J., so she started the conversation by telling Marva about the lack of communication with Fletch.

Marva smiled. "That's tough, honey. I remember when Jerry, my boys' father, first walked out on us. I was so lonely and depressed. Now, I know your husband hasn't walked out on you, but you probably feel lonely too. Maybe you're even homesick for your husband and family."

"I guess you're right. I've never been away from home or Fletch more than a few days at a time. I need that family support in my life."

Marva put down her rolling pin and came over to where Gen was sitting on a kitchen stool and gave her a hug. "Consider us your family while you're here," Marva offered.

Gen's eyes welled up with tears. "Thanks. You remind me of my mother. She is so domestic and all about family."

"Good." Marva smiled. "If I had a daughter, I'd like her to be like you. Now, just talk away. I'm a cheap shrink."

Marva laughed, and so did Gen.

They chatted about school, about raising kids, and about faith in a higher power. Gen was feeling better as she ate the baked pie-dough scraps, sprinkled with sugar and cinnamon, that Marva had made. Life was starting to look a little better with each bite.

"I sometimes get depressed too," Marva confessed. "Benny is slow, and he sometimes gets upset when he can't do certain things, but Bernie, who's much brighter, has been a problem at times too."

"In what way?" Gen asked.

"Well, as a kid, he often did impulsive things—you know, not stopping to think about the consequences of his actions. He was into more trouble in school than Benny was, and sometimes Bernie got Benny involved in some of his mischief."

"What do you mean?" Gen asked.

"Bernie sent a nasty note to one of his female high school teachers once. He got Benny to write it, so the teacher would blame Benny. But the teacher was smart enough to figure out who was behind the note."

"What was the note about?" Gen asked.

"Oh, just some teenage nonsense about loving the teacher—you know, a student crush. But I guess Bernie got a little specific about his feelings."

"What happened then?"

"Nothing much. We all had to go see the principal, and he made the boys apologize to the teacher. The whole matter was dropped."

"Who was the principal?"

"Haugen. He's been here for over ten years."

"Oh." *So that's Haugen's method of problem solving: an apology and it's all over. Maybe if Bernie had been given some professional help at that time, he wouldn't be accused of sexually molesting his patients now.*

Gen changed the subject. She could see that Marva was uncomfortable talking about Bernie's problems. "Do you ever go up into the attic at night? I've heard noise above my room on some nights."

Marva looked surprised but answered Gen's question. "Sometimes I go up there to find things or sit and reminisce about past days by looking at some old pictures or something."

Just then, Benny burst into the kitchen, carrying the framed photos Gen had requested. He proudly set the pictures in front of her.

Gen was pleasantly surprised. "These are awesome, Benny. I love them. Fletch will love them too. You did them so quickly. You must have spent all your spare time the past three days working on these."

"Not all my time. I did my chores too," Benny assured Gen while looking at his mother.

"I'm sure you did." Gen smiled. "You'll have to decide what price you want for these, and I'll pay you when I get my check in a few weeks."

"I'll do that," Benny said. "If it's okay with you, I'll keep them in my workshop through the weekend. I want to show Bernie when he comes home this weekend."

Gen nodded and looked at Marva. "Bernie's going to be home this weekend?" she asked.

"I guess so." Marva shrugged. "He called Benny last night. I'm not sure why he's coming home so much lately. I guess the dentistry business is slow."

I'll have to get hold of Fletch. This should bring him north, Gen thought. *I need my husband this weekend, for more than protection against Bernie.*

"I'm going upstairs and getting freshened up for supper," Gen announced. "Thanks for the chat, Marva. I feel better now."

"Good!"Anytime you want to talk, I'll be here," Marva said, turning the chicken pieces that were browning in the frying pan.

* * *

"Thank God I got hold of you," Gen said when Fletch picked up the phone.

"I'm sorry I didn't call for three days, but like I told you, I was going to Dallas and didn't want to pay roaming costs on my cell. I thought we could manage for three days."

"I know, sweetheart. I'm sorry if I sounded so desperate, but everything has been going wrong this week. I really need you here."

Gen told Fletch about Haugen, the senior boys, and Bernie's homecoming this weekend. Fletch promised to leave on Friday afternoon and be in Little Beaver late Friday night.

After Fletch told Gen all about his trip to Dallas, she asked him if his bank still had some good used computers for sale that they had replaced with newer models last fall.

"I think so," he said. "I'll check it out. Why do you ask?"

"My landlady's son wants a computer badly. He doesn't need a new one, just one that works and has a photo-manipulation program on it. Benny is into taking photos of the area wildlife and scenery, and he does a wonderful job. I'd like to get him a computer that will print some of these pictures for him, so he can see how they look without running to Bemidji to get them printed."

"I'll see what I can find. If I find anything good and inexpensive, I'll bring it along and set it up for Benny this weekend, okay?"

"You are a sweetheart. I love you so much and miss you terribly. I can't wait until the weekend," Gen said wistfully.

They talked and talked about trivial things. Gen didn't want to let him go.

"Supper's ready." Benny's voice was loud and clear coming up the stairway.

"Coming," Gen called back. "I've got to go, Fletch. Thanks for the nice visit. Love you and can't wait until you get here."

She hung up the phone and went to supper. The whole world seemed a little better now. Fletch had a way of making her feel safe and happy.

* * *

Thursday produced a light at the end of the dark tunnel.

Haugen came into the teachers' lounge at eight and asked Gen to stop into his office before school started. She grabbed her cup of coffee and followed him out the door.

"Sit down, Mrs. Fletcher," he said when she entered the office. "I think we've made some progress on your problem."

My problem! she thought. *How has this become my problem?*

"Superintendent Gray and I have conferred and decided we'll turn the papers over to the county sheriff. We don't want to be accused of withholding evidence on a possible murder investigation. The sheriff will set a time to interview you. Since you have been working with the two senior boys, you should be the one to explain these papers to the sheriff." Haugen smiled as he handed the original paragraphs to Gen.

The prick! Gen thought, grabbing the papers. *He doesn't even want to be there when I'm questioned. What a wimp! He's afraid that anything he'll say could come back to haunt him, so he's not saying a word.*

Gen sat silently, glaring at Haugen, waiting for him to speak.

"The boys will be notified too. Since they are both eighteen, their parents don't have to be present. If they want their parents at the interview, I'll see to it that the parents are notified."

That's big of you, Gen thought. Then she asked Haugen, "Do you mean that the two kids and I will be solely responsible for what goes down at these interviews?" Gen was noticeably irritated at Haugen's demeanor and lack of leadership.

"I guess so. The school doesn't want to get involved. It could get messy, you know."

"Yes, I know!" Gen said sharply.

"Now, Mrs. Fletcher, calm yourself. You don't want the school to spend valuable time on a murder investigation when we need that precious time to plan for the education of our students, do you?" Haugen smiled his "got-ya smile."

Gen got up, turned her back on Haugen, and marched out of the office to her room. Now she was mad—danged mad. *I'll show that wimp!*

Gen fumed most of the school day. She tried to control her anger for the sake of the students. Her outside demeanor was calm, but she was sick to her stomach inside.

After school, when Millie appeared in the doorway and asked, "Want to come for a drink?" Gen answered, "You bet I do—maybe even two!"

* * *

"That is so like Haugen," Millie said after Gen told her about the meeting in the office that morning. "What are you going to do?"

"I'll do the right thing. I'll talk to Sheriff Schultz and give him the papers. The only problem is that the sheriff is just as incompetent as Haugen. But I've done my duty—even if I never teach again."

"Relax! You're right about the incompetence of Haugen and Schultz. This may work in your favor. I doubt anything will ever come of all this. No one here has the knowledge to figure this out. Chances are it's all going to be swept under the rug and forgotten."

Gen gave Millie a skeptical look.

Millie raised her beer for a toast. "Here's to incompetence. May it ever flourish in Little Beaver, Minnesota."

Gen burst out with a hearty belly laugh that came from the bottom of her soul. "I'll drink to that!" she concurred, feeling really good for the first time in five days.

CHAPTER 16

My mama always said life was like a box of chocolates.
You never know what you're gonna get.
--Forrest Gump (1994)

The bar scene hadn't changed since last week. Charlie was still on his bar stool, and the place was full of Little Beaver citizens having a drink before supper.

Gen and Millie ordered another beer and were discussing school problems when D.J. entered the bar and made a beeline for their table.

"Good afternoon, ladies. Mind if I sit here?"

"Suit yourself," Millie said coldly.

Gen shrugged with an I-don't-care look on her face.

"What's new?" D.J. asked, trying to sound upbeat.

"Not much," Gen said. "Evie is still the main topic of conversation in Little Beaver, and graduation is high on the list of exciting things going on at the school. As senior class advisor, I'm in charge."

Millie excused herself and got up to leave. "I'm going to say hi to Charlie."

"Why have you been ignoring me?" D.J. asked once Millie was out of hearing range.

"I haven't been ignoring you," Gen whispered. "I've been busy."

"Yah, sure!" D.J. said sarcastically. "Have I made some sort of faux pas?" he asked, motioning Ed to bring over a beer.

"No. I just feel …" Gen hesitated. "Let's just forget Saturday, okay?"

"Okay, forget it if you like. I'll keep that memory if you don't mind."

"Suit yourself."

There was a moment of silence, and then Gen asked, "Whatever happened to that bone Hunter found?"

D.J. looked surprised. "Who told you?"

"It was a topic of conversation on Monday night at this bar. I don't remember who told me."

D.J. shrugged and smiled. "So much for keeping details about the investigation secret. The bone turned out to be an old one dug up by some animal, I guess. Maybe it came from the old Indian burial grounds near my farm."

"Yeah, that's what Graywolfe suggested on Monday. I guess he was right. Maybe he should be in charge of this investigation."

D.J. nodded in agreement. "Speak of the devil." D.J. pointed to the sheriff, who had just entered the bar.

"And the devil will appear," Gen whispered, as the sheriff spotted her and started walking toward her table.

"Good afternoon, Mrs. Fletcher. I hear you have a problem."

"I don't have a problem!" Gen said crisply. "You and the school have a problem."

"Whatever." The sheriff dismissed her assertive statement. He paused a moment, like he was wondering what to say next. "When can we talk about this?" he finally asked.

"Whenever you have time—in private, I hope, and when I'm not at school."

"Okay. How about tomorrow morning at seven at the Bumblebee Inn? I'm sure Mrs. Jacobs will give us some privacy."

"Sounds good," Gen said. "I'll be there."

The sheriff nodded and moved on to a different table.

Gen turned her attention to D.J. and asked, "Have Gretchen and Heidi had their puppies yet? My husband is coming this weekend, and he's interested in hunting dogs. If you're available, maybe we could come out and look at what you've got."

"Always glad to show my dogs, and yes, Gretchen had six puppies yesterday. Cutest little rascals you've ever seen—all black and white."

Gen smiled. "I'll bet they are. I'll call Fletch when I get home and tell him."

There was another moment of silence as both parties wondered what to say next. "I should go," Gen said. "I've got lesson plans to do, and I should prepare for my interview with Sheriff Schultz."

"Nothing to prepare for; just tell the truth."

"All I have is some information. Someone else is going to have to find out the truth."

"Okay, I'm sure our local law enforcement will get to the bottom of this in record time," D.J. said calmly, with a hint of irony in his voice.

Gen raised her eyebrows and shook her head in dismay as she stood up to leave. "See you. Hi to Hunter," she said as she walked away.

* * *

There was a chill in the air as Gen walked the two blocks back to the inn. She noticed a SUV sitting in front of the house. *I wonder who that is,* she thought.

Entering the living room from the front porch, Gen saw two middle-aged people sitting stiffly on the couch, talking to Marva.

"Sorry to interrupt," Gen said.

"It's quite all right, sweetie," Marva said. "These are Evie's parents, Linda and Brian Becker." Marva looked at the parents and said, "This is Genevieve Fletcher; she's the teacher who's teaching Evie's classes."

"Glad to meet you," Linda said, holding out her hand. She was a short woman, perfectly made up and coiffed. Gen shook the welcoming hand.

Brian sat looking straight ahead. It was plain to see he didn't want to be where he was. He was also short, with thinning gray hair and a mouth that turned down at either end.

Gen sat down on a chair near the couch to join the conversation. *He looks like a man who could sexually abuse a stepdaughter*, she thought.

"I'm so worried about Evie," Linda said. "Maybe you could shed some light on this situation, Gen?"

"I don't know much except what I've heard around town," Gen lied. She didn't want to say anything about the senior boys' papers. "I knew Evie in college. We lived in the same dorm for a year. We weren't good friends, but I saw her around. I hope she's safe somewhere."

"We do too." Linda gave a faint smile. "Evie made several phone calls home a week before she disappeared. She told us she was unhappy with the way things were going at the school. It almost sounded like she was off her meds again."

"What meds did she take?" Gen asked.

"Something for depression. Evie has been taking a variety of drugs for depression since she was a teenager."

"That's not good, since she also drank a lot of alcohol," Gen said. "Alcohol and depression drugs sort of contradict each other."

"Yes, I told her that many times. She wouldn't listen," Linda said sadly.

"She never listened to anything anyone told her." Brian's voice dripped with sarcasm.

Gen changed the subject. "Did she ever mention anyone named Joe?"

"Joe?" Linda pondered for a moment. "I don't remember a Joe, but then Evie had lots of boyfriends, one after another, since she was fifteen."

"Too many," Brian added.

"Well, this Joe—it seems—lives in Seattle. Maybe an old friend from her college days who moved out west?"

"I can't recall anything like that," Linda said.

"The sheriff will be here at five to question the Beckers," Marva said. "You can help me in the kitchen, Gen, when he gets here. I'm sure the Beckers will want some privacy."

The parents nodded.

"And of course you'll stay for supper," Marva stated. "There aren't many places in town to get a good meal, and I'd love to have you. I'm very fond of Evie. She's a lovely girl."

"You're so kind," Linda said with tears welling up in her eyes. "I hope it isn't too much of an imposition."

"None at all," Marva said with a smile. Then she changed the subject, trying to make small talk until the sheriff arrived. "So, how was your trip from Moorhead?"

"Good," both Beckers answered at once.

There was a moment of silence followed by a knock on the door. "That must be the sheriff," Marva said, getting up to answer the door.

Sheriff Schultz entered with an air of self-confidence and authority. The Beckers seemed impressed as Marva introduced them to the sheriff. Then she excused herself and motioned for Gen to follow her into the kitchen.

"I wonder what he's asking them," Gen whispered when Marva handed her a bunch of carrots to clean for supper.

"Probably nothing of much importance," Marva said. "But maybe he can answer some of their questions and calm their fears."

"Maybe," Gen agreed.

"Since the Beckers are staying for supper, we'll put another potato in the pot and cut the swiss steak pieces in half. I'm sure we'll have enough for all," Marva said.

Gen smiled. *Just like my mother. Nobody ever left the farm hungry.*

* * *

At the supper table, the conversation remained general and friendly. Linda was very talkative; Brian ate. Linda seemed nervous and fragile at times; Brian remained haughty and distant. Oscar sat silently and ate. Marva was full of information and kind thoughts. Gen listened, trying to catch something that might help solve the mystery.

"I liked Miss Evie," Benny burst out in his usual open and friendly manner when there was a lull in the conversation. "She said she liked me. I'm sorry she left."

"I'm sure she liked you, too, Benny," Linda said. "Evie is always open and friendly to all people. Did she ever say anything to you about leaving?"

"No way," Benny answered curtly and continued eating.

"Maybe her depression got the best of her," Gen said. "Maybe she just had to leave—you know, a change in scenery. I'm sure she's okay, and after she's had some time to relax and think this whole thing through, she'll call or come home."

Linda smiled and seemed relieved. "You know, the sheriff said the same thing. I'm sure he knows what he's talking about."

Gen looked knowingly at Marva and Oscar. She could see doubt written all over their faces. They both nodded as a unit, and in an attempt to appease Linda, she found herself joining them.

CHAPTER 17

Love means never having to say you're sorry.
—*Love Story* (1970)

The next morning, Gen woke up in time for breakfast and to say good-bye to the Beckers.

"Have a safe trip home. I know they'll find Evie soon," Gen assured Linda.

"I'm sure they will." Linda smiled. "If only she'd come home Easter weekend, this wouldn't have happened."

"Wasn't she planning to come home?" Gen asked.

"No. She called and told us she had other plans for the weekend. We always picked her up for vacations. She didn't have a car, you know."

"Yes, I've heard that." *If she knew she wasn't going home over Easter and had other plans, maybe she planned this whole disappearing act.* Gen pondered the mystery. *But how did she get out of town undetected when she didn't own a car? She surely didn't walk to the nearest town without anyone seeing her. Unless she did it at night. I'll have to ask Marva if they heard Evie come home on Friday night.*

"Well, nice meeting you," Linda said, interrupting Gen's thought process. Linda gave Gen a big hug. Brian shook hands.

Gen went to her room and got ready for her interview with the sheriff and then school.

Sheriff Schultz was at the inn promptly at seven thirty. His one claim to fame was that you could count on him to be prompt.

"Good morning," he said in an official tone of voice when Gen opened the front door. He had his notepad and pencil in hand.

"Good morning, Sheriff," Gen answered cheerfully. "I see you're all ready for a day of super sleuthing."

"Sure am, after I interview you, Mrs. Fletcher." He paused a moment. "Is there somewhere we can sit?"

Gen pointed to the living room and then led the way. She sat down in a large stuffed chair. The sheriff chose the couch.

"So," he began, "the principal told me you had some information for me that might help in my investigation of the Evelyn Pretsler case?"

"Yes, I do." Gen handed him the papers the two senior boys had written. The sheriff read both, taking his time. He showed no reaction while reading the material.

Gen sat patiently and waited until he had finished.

"Well, this certainly sheds a whole new light on the case. It looks like Evelyn had a good reason to disappear. Maybe these boys were blackmailing her—threatening to expose her. What do you think, Mrs. Fletcher?"

"I think you may have something there. Now all you've got to do is figure out how she got out of town undetected the night she disappeared. Since she didn't have a car, maybe somebody drove her. Maybe that somebody knows where she went or killed her."

The sheriff nodded. "I'll keep these papers for evidence. I'll also question the two seniors involved. Once they know the seriousness of their statements in these papers, they'll come clean." He seemed really sure of himself.

"I hope you're right." *He doesn't know how tight-mouthed these kids can be. Oh well, it's his problem now.*

School went really well on Friday. Danny and Allen were absent. Gen enjoyed the classroom discussions, which were getting louder and more intense. The students seemed to take pride in what they had to say and in giving their opinions on a topic. The seniors had filled out all types of forms that week and seemed happy that their lives were more organized and taking some direction for the summer and fall. Things were looking up.

* * *

Gen rushed home after school on Friday, feeling like a kid anticipating a visit from her grandparents. She took the stairs to her bedroom two at a time. She wanted to get all her schoolwork done and freshen up before Fletch got there, so they could have the whole weekend together doing things they wanted to do and not worrying about work.

"My, you look pretty," Oscar teased at supper. "Expecting anyone special?"

Gen blushed. "Who told you?"

"A little bird," Oscar answered with a wink at Marva.

"Yah sure!" Gen said with a nervous giggle. She felt like a schoolgirl being teased on her first date. *Has it been that long?*

Gen helped Oscar and Marva with the dishes and then went to her room to read for a while. She glanced at the clock on the wall. *Eight o'clock; he should be here soon.*

She went downstairs to watch some TV. The whole family had disappeared. *They must have gone to play cards at the café,* she thought. She turned on the TV and searched the channels until she found TCM. She liked old, romantic movies best.

At ten minutes to nine, there was a commotion at the front door. Gen rushed to open it. To her surprise a young man who looked like Benny stood there with a big grin on his face.

"Well," he said with delight, "either my mother has gotten a lot younger and prettier or I'm looking at Mrs. Fletcher."

Gen nodded and gave him a curious smile. "You must be Bernie."

"You're right!"

He picked up his large duffel bag and went directly to Benny's room. Then he returned to the living room empty-handed. "Where is everyone?" he asked.

"They've all gone to play cards at the café, I think. But they'll be back shortly," she added, so he wouldn't think she would be here all alone for long. "I guess I was too busy with my own thoughts at supper to ask what they were doing tonight."

"That's fine. I'll talk to you." He smiled. "So tell me, what do people usually call you?"

"Gen, short for Genevieve."

"Okay, Gen, what are your plans for the weekend?"

"My husband will be here shortly. I'll be showing him the sights in and around Little Beaver, and maybe we'll go scouting in the area. He likes the great outdoors—quite a hunter, dontcha know."

Bernie looked disappointed. "No, I don't know." He paused a moment. "You picked up the 'dontcha know' thing, I see. It's really catching. Everyone uses it up here."

"Yah-sure, ya-betcha," she teased, feeling a bit more relaxed.

Bernie laughed too. There was a moment of silence.

"Well," he said with a resigned sigh, "until Mr. Fletcher gets here, tell me all about yourself. Where were you educated?"

"Moorhead State. So was Fletch—that's what everyone calls my husband." She was a bit nervous talking to Bernie, but he seemed surprisingly congenial, not at all lecherous like she'd imagined him. *Perhaps all the accusations against him are false, or maybe all this charm is just a cover-up for his dark side.*

"You said you had supper? I'm starved. Do you suppose Mom left something in the kitchen for me and Fletch? Not many places to eat after you pass Bemidji. The Red Lake reservation shuts down at six, and so does Little Fork, which is just as well, since they don't even have a decent fast-food place there."

"I guess the lack of population up here causes a lack of businesses, including eating places," Gen speculated.

"You're right. Come with me and help me scout out the kitchen. My mom is a terrific cook."

"You're right about that. She reminds me of my own mom—very domestic, all about family, and a terrific cook."

Bernie nodded in agreement and led the way to the kitchen.

He found some leftover fried chicken, potato salad, and apple pie, which he set out on the counter, along with a plate and fork. He poured himself a cup of milk, sat down on a stool by the counter, and began eating.

Gen sat on a stool opposite Bernie, watching him closely as they made small talk between Bernie's mouthfuls of food. He was hungry and ate heartily.

That's how Fletch found them when he entered the kitchen—Bernie eating and Gen watching.

"Anyone home?" Fletch asked, sporting his omnipresent grin. "The TV's on so loud, you didn't hear me knock."

"Fletch!" Gen turned around on her stool. She jumped up, ran to him, threw her arms around him, and kissed him. She clung to him and wouldn't let go, kissing him all over his face.

Bernie cleared his throat while watching the lovebirds. "Maybe you should introduce me to the guy you're kissing?" he asked.

Gen came back down to earth. "Oh, sorry. Bernie Jacobs, this is my husband, Evan—called Fletch by everyone."

"Hi, Fletch." Bernie waved, holding a chicken drumstick. "Mind if I continue eating while you two carry on?"

"Not at all." Fletch smiled. "Is it all right if I join you?"

Fletch sat next to Bernie on a stool while Gen got a plate and fork from the cupboard. Both men ate heartily while discussing northern Minnesota's scenery, roads, and wildlife. It seemed both enjoyed hunting.

So much for a romantic evening, Gen thought as she watched the men talk and enjoy their food.

* * *

"He doesn't seem so bad!" Fletch said, lying in bed next to Gen as she cuddled in his arms. "Looks like a regular guy to me."

"Yes, I agree. Maybe all that charm and personality is just a cover-up for a darker side."

"Oh, I don't know. He seems okay to me."

"Then how do you explain all those pictures in the attic of nude women in odd poses. He either bought those pictures from someone else or took them himself."

"I don't know how you explain it. I'm no psychiatrist. He could have developed that friendly chairside manor for his dentistry practice. Dentists have to learn how to make pleasant small talk while they torture you."

Fletch laughed at his own joke.

"That's not funny!" Gen poked his arm. "If he's got a lecherous side concerning women, he needs help."

"I guess you're right, babe. Let's not talk about Bernie. I want to love you all night long."

* * *

Pewter clouds hid the morning sun when the couple emerged from the inn for a morning walk. They had decided to wait until after their walk to eat breakfast. Since they didn't spend much time during the night discussing the Evie case, Gen filled Fletch in on all the details she'd learned during her two weeks in Little Beaver. She summed up her knowledge with: "In my opinion, Evie planned this whole thing. She will probably end up in prison for child sexual molestation if they ever find her."

"Sounds like you and the sheriff have figured this thing out. I've just got three questions: Why did she hide or destroy her record books? Why did she throw her cell phone away with information on it? And who in the heck is Joe?"

"All good questions, my dear Watson." Gen said using her best British accent.

"This all seems to get Bernie off the hook. Maybe he's just a secret pervert and has nothing to do with the Evie case."

"I hope, for Marva's sake, that he's no pervert of any kind. I hope there's some explanation for those pictures and those accusations by his patients."

"I hope so too."

"In the meantime, let's just drop the Evie case for today. I just want to enjoy the day, take in the scenery, and continue being madly in love with you."

Fletch kissed her gently on her lips. "Okay, babe, sounds good to me."

CHAPTER 18

You can't handle the truth!
—*A Few Good Men* (1992)

Marva and Oscar were in the kitchen having a second cup of coffee when Gen and Fletch returned from their morning walk.

"What a beautiful day it's turning out to be," Gen said. "We thought it might rain, but it's clearing off nicely."

Oscar nodded in agreement and said, "Are you two ready for some breakfast, or are you going to live on love this weekend?"

Everyone laughed.

"We won't starve," Gen said. "Fletch filled up on Marva's leftover chicken, potato salad, and pie last night before we went to bed."

"Well, sit down. We'll make you some breakfast," Marva offered. "Oscar can make the pancakes, and I'll do some eggs and sausage."

The two cooks got busy while Gen and Fletch told them about the wildlife they'd spotted down by the lake on their walk. Talking about wildlife made Gen think of the twin brothers. "Where are Benny and Bernie this morning?"

"Out walking. Benny wanted to take some more pictures," Marva answered.

"We've got something for Benny," Fletch said. "I'll set it up after we finish our breakfast."

"Set it up?" Marva asked. She paused a moment and then asked, "Is it a computer?"

"Yup," Fletch said.

"He'll love it! Thank you so much," Marva squealed with delight as she loaded Fletch's plate with food and set it before him. "Bon appétit."

As promised, when they finished eating, the Fletchers went out to the pickup and brought in all the computer components.

Oscar helped Fletch set up the computer. By the time the twins got home from their walk, all was ready.

Benny burst through the door. "Guess what, Mom? We saw a mother moose and her two little ones by the lake. I got some neat pictures. Bernie helped. He advised me."

Bernie grinned. "Benny has a good eye for this type of thing. I didn't need to give him any advice."

Benny grinned from ear to ear at the compliment from the brother he worshiped.

"Go to your bedroom," Marva said. "There's a surprise for you."

Benny rushed to his bedroom, followed closely by Bernie.

"Wow!" Benny shrieked. "That's awesome! Where did the computer come from?"

Marva was standing by the bedroom door, peeking in. "From the Fletchers," she said.

Benny raced from the bedroom into the kitchen, grabbed Gen, and gave her a big hug. "Thanks, thanks, thanks," he said over and over.

When he released her, Gen caught her breath. "Fletch was the one who brought it and set it up."

Benny paused a moment, looked shyly at Fletch, and pondered what he should do next. Then he grabbed Fletch and gave him a big hug. "Thank you so much," he said.

"You're welcome," Fletch answered with a smile.

Benny went back to the bedroom, where Bernie and Oscar were playing with the computer. The three spent the next hour trying the different programs on the computer and also running off some of Benny's latest photos.

"Thanks so much," Marva said with tears in her eyes. "You made his day. What do we owe you?" she asked the Fletchers.

"Nothing," Fletch said. "It's a secondhand computer from the bank. I got it cheap—really cheap. The programs I put into it were some of mine, so nothing cost much. Let's just consider that chicken, potato salad, pie, eggs, pancakes, and sausage I've been eating as full payment."

Marva hugged Fletch. "You're so kind to think of Benny."

"It was Gen's idea. I think she's grown really fond of you all."

"Good. We all love her. She tries so hard at the school to help all the kids. I've heard many good reports from the ladies at the church."

Gen smiled and changed the subject. "Why don't I call D.J. and see if we can come look at his dogs sometime this weekend. Then we'll plan the rest of the weekend."

"Good idea," Fletch replied.

While Marva and Fletch talked about banking and CDs, Gen went to the living room and called D.J.

"We can come Sunday morning around ten," she said, returning to the kitchen. "He's on his way to Bemidji now to get some supplies and won't be back until late tonight." She paused a moment. "So, why don't we take a trip up to International Falls, I've always wanted to see the coldest spot in the United States."

"It's beautiful up that way right now," Marva said. "Just follow the gravel road that goes through Little Beaver east until you hit Highway 53 North. You can't miss it."

"Sounds good," Fletch said. "Thanks for breakfast. We'll be back later tonight; save the leftovers."

* * *

All the walking and fresh air made the Fletchers very tired. During their trip up north, they explored many nature paths and pristine wooded areas that had not been diluted by human presence.

After they raided the refrigerator, when they got home around seven thirty, they went to bed and fell asleep quickly.

The family was really quiet when they got home from the special church program, so they wouldn't wake up the Fletchers.

"What's that?" Gen sat up in bed. A loud bang had awakened her.

"What's wrong?" Fletch asked, rubbing the sleep out of his eyes.

"I heard something—a bang. It sounded like something fell on the roof of the house."

"What time is it anyway?" Fletch asked, looking at his wristwatch that glowed in the dark. "Jeez, Gen, it's one o'clock."

"Shush," Gen whispered.

They both sat quietly in bed listening. After a few seconds, they heard noises coming from above them. "Someone is up in the attic again," Gen said. "They must have knocked something over or dropped something. Maybe it's Bernie looking through his pictures."

"Let's go see," Fletch suggested.

"No, we can't do that!"

"Why not?"

"It's none of our business."

"Oh, for God's sake. We'll never find out what's going on if we don't ask!"

"Well, I guess you're right. What if he's got a gun?"

"Gun? Your imagination is really too much at times, Gen. Why would he take a gun with him to look at pictures in the attic?"

"Oh, I don't know." Gen was irritated. "Okay, let's go. You lead the way."

The two got out of bed, grabbed a flashlight, and stealthily opened the attic door and crept up the steep stairway. When they got to the top, they found a surprised Bernie looking through his trunk.

"What's going on?" Fletch asked. "It's one o'clock in the morning."

"I'm just looking at some of my old pictures," Bernie answered calmly.

"I've seen those pictures. Sorry, I snooped. They are not nice pictures!" Gen said emphatically.

"I know," Bernie said apologetically. "I was wondering what I should do with them."

"You should be ashamed, taking such pictures," Gen scolded.

"They're not mine!" Benny said emphatically. "They belong to my boss."

"What?" Gen exclaimed. "Why in the world would you store your boss's pictures?"

"Because he asked me to. He kind of hinted I'd be out of a job if I didn't," Bernie answered.

"That's terrible. You can sue him for that. He has no right to threaten your job if you don't do illegal things for him. Minnesota is a union state. There must be something in worker's-rights laws about that," Fletch said.

"Well, I know, but—dental jobs are hard to find." Bernie was making excuses for his behavior.

"Bernie, we know about the lawsuit against you concerning some improper behavior toward female patients," Fletch said. "Do you suppose your boss used that to get you to store his pictures?"

"Maybe. He's had some charges made against him too, a few years ago, but he said he took care of it. I guess he paid the patients off. He said he'd take care of my charges too."

Fletch looked skeptical. "This is sounding like a scheme by patients to extract money from you dentists. I think you should report all this and let the chips fall where they may. This could go on and on, you know."

Bernie hung his head. "I know."

Fletch looked at Bernie with sympathy. "Did you make inappropriate comments to your patients?" he asked.

"Not really. I just did what my boss told me. He said to be friendly to patients and make small talk. He also said today's modern patients don't mind a spicy story now and then. I didn't think the stories I told were so bad. I tell the same stories to my mom, and she laughs. I also call patients sweetheart or honey now and then. I don't mean to be flirtatious; I just don't always remember their names."

"Well, that kind of thing can cause problems in the modern workplace," Fletch said. "It's unfortunate but true. You got some bad advice from your boss. If he has patients that want to cause trouble or blackmail the dentists, that type of talk and behavior can be used against you. Sorry, Bernie, but I think you fell into a pile of dung. The best thing to do now is report all this and hope the judicial system can figure it all out and do the right thing."

"You're probably right," Bernie said sadly. "I really need this job to help my mom and Benny, and also to pay off my college debts. I feel like I've let my family down. I don't want Mom to know what's happening—she'd worry."

"Your mom knows," Gen said. "She hasn't come right out and said it, but I've heard her up here at night, and she told me she'd been looking at old pictures. I'm pretty sure she's gone through this trunk."

"Oh no," Bernie moaned. He paused a moment. "I'm sorry this all happened," he said, hanging his head in shame. "I should have known better. I'm such a dumb country bumpkin."

"You're young, maybe a little naïve, but that's no reason you should be conned by your boss and some greedy patients." Fletch assured Benny. "I know a good lawyer in Minneapolis. He's a good friend I went to school with. He does this type of thing. I can call him, and he can advise you."

"I can't afford a lawyer. Neither can my mom," Bernie said sadly.

"That's why we have public defenders," Fletch said.

Bernie stood silently, thinking for a moment. "I guess you're right. The longer I let this thing fester, the worse it will get."

"Do you want me to call my lawyer friend?" Fletch asked.

"Okay," Bernie agreed reluctantly. "Thanks."

"I'll call my friend on Monday, when I get back to St. Cloud. In the meantime, you take those pictures back to your boss and tell him you're not storing them anymore. The legal system will have to take it from there."

"Should I tell my mom, Benny, and Oscar?" Bernie asked.

"Yes, I think that would be for the best," Fletch said. "The truth is always a good path to follow. If you're telling the truth, you won't get your stories mixed up every time you tell them."

There was a moment of silence. "I'll do that in the morning," Bernie said. "I don't want to wake everyone up in the middle of the night." He paused a moment. "Will you two help me?"

"Sure we will," the Fletchers said together.

CHAPTER 19

I'm the king of the world!
—*Titanic* (1997)

Gen and Fletch slept in on Sunday morning. By the time they got up, the Jacobs entourage had gone to early church. Gen made scrambled eggs and toast. Then she called D.J. to make sure he was up and ready for them. At nine thirty they drove out to D.J's place. They used Fletch's pickup, because on the gravel road, the trip would not be feasible in a small car.

D.J. was standing on the porch when they drove up. "Welcome to my world," he called as they got out of the pickup.

Gen introduced the men. "D.J., this is Fletch; Fletch, D.J."

"Beautiful country out here!" Fletch said, shaking hands with D.J.

"I like it." D.J. smiled. "Gen has told me some things about you, Fletch. I hear you like to hunt."

"Love it. My buddies and I like to hunt waterfowl as well as game birds. We also do some deer hunting in the fall. My next goal is to bag a moose."

D.J. smiled. "We've got lots of moose around here. I don't mind if people shoot a few. They can be very destructive—mean too. Come on in. I've got the coffeepot on."

"Nice cabin," Fletch said as they entered the cabin. "This looks like a man cave."

"I guess it is, since there are no women around here."

The Fletchers took seats at the only table in the room, while D.J. got cups and the coffeepot.

"So how are Gretchen's puppies doing?" Gen asked.

"They're doing fine—growing like weeds. Heidi had her litter yesterday morning. She had five; one's dark brown and white, so now I have eleven to sell."

"Tell me," Fletch asked, "do you also train these dogs?"

"Yes, I do. I'll sell them as three-month-old puppies, but I don't recommend that. People that don't know how to train a dog will end up giving the dog away or putting it into a shelter. I don't want that to happen to my dogs. So you better know what you're doing if you get a puppy."

D.J. paused a moment and then added, "If a dog is properly trained, you will be in charge; if he's not properly trained, he'll be in charge. It's not much fun having an eighty-pound dog run your life."

Fletch nodded. "So when do you start weaning these puppies from their mothers?"

"At about four weeks. The process is usually completed at eight weeks. Puppies can learn important behavior from their moms and littermates, such as how to interpret signs of dominance, inhibit their own biting habits, and submit to dominant dogs. It's good for the mothers to slowly dry up their milk supply too. Weaning can be a stressful time for mothers and puppies, so it should be done with proper supervision. That's why I never sell my puppies until they are about twelve weeks old. When I train them, I sell them at around a year old. It depends on the dog and how well he trained."

"How hard is it to train a dog?" Fletch asked.

"Training a puppy starts with a daily routine. Such things as where his food and water dish are located, when he eats, where he sleeps, where to potty, and when he plays are important. You also have to teach words like 'no' and 'good.' This should all start at two or three months of age. Don't rely on food treats to train. If you do, the puppy won't listen unless he's hungry. Rely on respect training—he must learn to listen to your words."

"Where do people usually keep these dogs?" Gen asked. She was concerned about a big dog roaming in their apartment.

"If you want to keep the dog indoors, you'll need a crate to put him in, because a crate is a valuable aid for potty training. It's also easier to travel with the dog. Mother dogs can help potty train their young. If you get a puppy at three months old, you'll need to start potty training him immediately. I use an exercise pen outdoors that the puppies get to through a dog door in my garage.

"You also have to socialize your puppy to get along with people and teach him your household rules." D.J. looked at Gen. "It's a lot like training a very young child. Think of your early-childhood classes in college."

Gen nodded.

"Enough talk," D.J. said with a smile. "Let's go look at the puppies."

Gen and Fletch followed D.J. to the shed, where he greeted his mother dogs with a friendly, "Good morning, sweethearts. How are my two favorite girls?"

Not a single bark was heard as the three humans entered the shed. The female dogs were well trained and knew D.J.'s scent and voice.

When Gen saw the puppies, she instantly fell in love. "Oh look, Fletch, they're so adorable. Can we have at least two?"

"Hold on, sweetie," Fletch cautioned. "The question isn't can we *have* them, it's can we *afford* them?"

Gen ignored her husband's comment as she opened the door to the pen where Gretchen and her puppies were housed. Gen sat down to play with the puppies. Gretchen seemed to accept the newcomer very well. A babysitter now and then suited her just fine.

D.J. let the two female dogs out of the pens and picked up two of Gretchen's puppies. "We'll put them outside on the grass to play and explore," he said. "The mothers can go for a run while we baby-sit."

Gen and Fletch each picked up two puppies and followed D.J. outdoors.

Everyone had a good time watching the puppies stumble around and sniff at things. They were still very young and spent their time trying to find their mother.

"What do you charge for a dog?" Fletch asked.

"Well, if I train them until they are around a year old, I ask $1,000. Puppies are only $400. These dogs can eat a lot as they grow, and they also take a lot of my time."

Fletch laughed. "I'll bet they do."

While the men talked business, Gen played with the puppies. Her maternal instincts kicked in, and she felt the need to hold, cuddle, and kiss them.

Fletch put in an order for one male dog, trained. "When you feel he's trained and ready to learn some hunting skills, call me. I'll come pick him up. Since you're the expert and you've met us, match one of the puppies to us. I trust your expertise."

The men shook hands, and D.J. walked the Fletchers to their pickup.

"See you," he said to Gen. "If you ever decide to quit teaching, let me know. You'd make a very good dog trainer. I can tell."

Gen smiled, and Fletch gave D.J. an inquisitive stare.

On the drive home, Fletch asked Gen, "What did he mean by inviting you to help him train his dogs?"

"I don't know," Gen lied.

Fletch looked at her a few moments and then dropped the subject.

* * *

The Jacobses and Oscar were having lunch—soup and sandwiches—when Gen and Fletch arrived back at the Bumblebee Inn.

"Sit down and eat," Marva invited, getting two more soup bowls and eating utensils.

"Glad to," Fletch said. "I don't know what it is up here in the wilds that gives me such a hearty appetite."

"Maybe it's not the wilds but the romance," Oscar teased.

"Maybe." Fletch chuckled.

While they were eating, Gen and Fletch kept looking at Bernie with inquisitive stares that said *Did you tell them?*

Bernie finally spoke. "We all talked to Pastor Johnson after the service about my problems. He recommended the same solutions that you did," Bernie assured the Fletchers.

Both Fletchers breathed a sigh of relief.

"I'm sorry I let you down, Mom," Bernie said sadly.

"Not at all," Marva comforted her son. "We all make mistakes. Benny and I will survive very nicely, with Oscar's help, while you solve your problems." She paused a moment. "Now, let's forget about it and enjoy our remaining time together."

Bernie smiled, but his body language still looked very depressed.

"Do you still want me to call my lawyer friend?" Fletch asked, checking to see if Bernie had changed his mind.

"Yes, that would be very nice of you," Bernie answered. "I don't know how I'll pay a lawyer, but I guess I need to have faith enough to believe that if I do the right thing—like Pastor Johnson said—everything will turn out okay."

"I'll help pay the lawyer with my picture sales," Benny said.

"I'm sure you will," Marva said, patting Benny's hand, doubt written on her face.

* * *

Gen and Fletch excused themselves and went upstairs. Fletch wanted to start for home around three.

They cuddled on the bed, made love, and talked about their future.

"I've got to go, babe." Fletch kissed his bride. "I need a good night's sleep. I've got a big meeting in the morning, and I need to be on top of my game."

"I know," Gen murmured.

"I feel better about you being up here alone, since I've met some of the people you hang out with," Fletch confessed. "I'm pretty sure Bernie isn't a murderer, and even D.J. seems to be a pretty good guy. Marva and Oscar are like a mother and dad to you. This is really a good place for you to stay."

"I know," Gen purred. "The only thing missing in my life is you."

"I miss my girl. It will all be over soon."

Fletch got up and packed his few belongings. They went downstairs and said good-bye beside the pickup. As Fletch drove away, Gen felt a deep sense of loss and loneliness. *Living apart is no way to have a good marriage*, she thought. *I'm just going to have to find a job closer to St. Cloud.*

Gen went back into the house, where Marva and Oscar were having a cup of coffee in the kitchen. "Where are Benny and Bernie?" she asked.

"Bernie left about two, and Benny is out in the shed, making picture frames. He's bound and determined to make a profitable business out of his pictures," Marva said with a sigh. "He told Bernie not to worry about anything. He'd support us with his picture sales and also help Bernie with the lawyer fees. I hope he succeeds. He'll be so disappointed if he doesn't."

Gen had an idea. "Maybe Liz at the convenience store could help him out. She might let him set up a display of his pictures and sell them at the store, if he does some work for her now and then. I'm sure if people see the pictures, they'll buy them."

Marva's eyes lit up. "I never thought of that. I'll talk to Liz in the morning."

"No," Gen said firmly, "let Benny do it. The more he does for himself, the more pride he'll have in his work and the better he'll do overall. That's the way it usually works."

"Gen is right," Oscar said, putting his hand over Marva's. "You need to step back and let him do this himself. I know it's hard; you're so protective of him, but he needs to take responsibility for his successes and failures. That's the way he'll become a man."

Marva looked at Oscar with love shining in her eyes. "I'll try."

Everyone sat quietly for a while, savoring the moment. Gen felt uncomfortable but wanted to continue with some obligatory chatter. *Maybe this would be a good time to ask them about Evie,* Gen thought. "By the way, did either one of you hear Evie come in on Good Friday, the night she disappeared?"

"Well, no," Marva said. "I'm deaf without my hearing aid, and I take it out at night. So I didn't hear anything."

"I didn't either," Oscar said. "I'm not deaf, but some think I'm getting there. I know I have the TV on a little loud. I didn't hear a thing."

"What about Benny?" Gen asked.

"The sheriff asked him that question, and he said no," Marva said. "He was very emphatic about it. I'm not sure what it is that's bothering him about Evie's disappearance, but whenever someone asks him about it, he gets irritated."

I'll have to question him and get to the bottom of this, Gen thought.

CHAPTER 20

Round up the usual suspects.
—*Casablanca* (1942)

The faculty in the teachers' lounge on Monday morning were sullen. They all seemed to be trying to get enough caffeine to be pumped up for the day. Gen sat quietly sipping from her steaming cup of coffee and reviewing her lesson plans for the week.

"Tough weekend?" Nick asked as he sat down next to her.

"No, just busy. My husband was here, so we were on the run all the time, trying to get as much done as possible."

"Ya-sure!" he teased.

Gen smiled and dropped the subject. "Did you notice if Haugen was in his office when you came in?" she asked.

"Now that you mention it, I think there was light in his office when I walked by. He probably is visiting with a parent or board member."

"Thanks, I'll check it out. I need to talk to him before classes start."

Gen finished her coffee and left the lounge. When she approached Haugen's office, she noticed two middle-aged women leaving. Gen waited until the women were out of sight; then she went to the office and knocked on the door.

"Come in," Haugen called from his desk.

"Good morning." Gen tried to sound fresh and enthusiastic. "I've got a problem I was wondering if you could help me with."

Haugen smiled. "Sit down, Mrs. Fletcher, and tell me what's on your mind."

"Well," Gen began, "last week the two boys who wrote those controversial papers were very sullen and aggressive. If looks could kill, I'd be dead."

"Sorry to hear that, but that's usually the kind of reaction you'll get from aggressive, unmotivated students when they've been challenged."

"Okay," Gen concurred, "now, what can I do about it? Would you talk to them?"

"No. I talked to them last week, and they must have told their mothers, because I just finished talking to a couple of very agitated women. They are ready to sue the school and prosecute Miss Pretsler because their children were abused here. This is all turning very nasty, and the law still hasn't a clue as to what happened to Evelyn. It would be easier to solve this problem if they could find our missing teacher and get her side of the story. I'm not sure the boys are telling the truth—at least not the whole truth. They are bending the facts to suit themselves."

"Okay. Now tell me what happened to all Miss Pretsler's records. The only records you gave me were her lesson plans for the following week after she disappeared. Did you ever find any other records? It would be nice if I knew what went on in her classes this year before I got here. It might also help clear up some of this mystery."

"What precisely do you want to know?" Haugen asked.

"Well, for starters, where are her grade books? It would be helpful for me to know what kinds of grades the kids got before I got here. It might also help us to understand what happened between Evelyn and the two senior boys. Some of the other students have told me bits and pieces about their behavior in classes and that they were both failing English before Evelyn started tutoring them."

"I don't know what happened to her grade book. Perhaps she destroyed all the records before she left. You can always look at the individual report cards of each student to see what kind of grades they were getting."

"That's a lot of work. It would be easier to have a record book with all the grades listed in one place."

"Well, Mrs. Fletcher, that seems to be impossible at this time. Those books are missing. I'd hoped you would find them somewhere in Evelyn's belongings."

Gen breathed a sigh of disgust. "Well, I haven't. She must have destroyed them. How could she do that? Did she burn them? Did she bury them?"

"Don't ask me." Haugen stared at Gen. "Miss Pretsler did some strange things. I don't follow my teachers around twenty-four/seven, so I don't always see what they are up to." Haugen's voice was rising in volume, and he was noticeably agitated.

Gen gave up. Haugen was obviously sandbagging, and this conversation was going nowhere. As she got up to leave, she said, "I'm sure if we find the records, we'd have an answer to Evelyn's disappearance."

"Well—" Haugen paused a moment. "I could agree with you, but then we'd both be wrong," he said with a smug look on his face.

Gen shook her head and left the office.

*　*　*

After her first senior English class, where Danny and Allen were still giving her looks of raw fury and aggression, the rest of the school day went well.

Gen stayed after school until five to finish some work. She knew the front door would be locked, so she decided to leave via the furnace room door.

As she entered the room, the janitor was just shutting things down for the night.

"Hello, Mr. Whitefield," Gen said. "Done for the day?"

"Yup," the middle-aged, overweight, slightly balding man replied. "Another day, another dollar."

He chuckled, and so did Gen.

He opened the furnace door and threw in the last batch of wastepaper he had collected from the rooms. The papers crackled in the fire and burned quickly.

Gen watched. She had a sudden revelation. "Did Evie Pretsler ever come in and out of this school through the furnace room?" she asked.

"All the time. She came over on weekends through this room. She did a lot of work here at night and on weekends."

"Do you remember if she was here late on the Thursday night before Good Friday when she disappeared?"

"Come to think of it, I believe she was the last teacher out that night. The reason I remember is because I was down here when she came through, having a cigarette before I went back upstairs to lock up for the long weekend. She stopped to talk. I finally excused myself and left. When I got back, she was gone. She was carrying a bag full of stuff. I'm not sure what was in it. Teachers often carry books and things home at night, dontcha know."

"Do teachers ever burn stuff in the furnace?"

"All the time. We don't have shredders in the school."

Gen smiled. *That could explain what happened to Evie's records.*

"Thanks for the information, Mr. Whitefield. See you around."

He nodded, and Gen left the building.

* * *

Gen entered the bar around five thirty and spied Millie at a table, talking to Sheriff Schultz. Millie motioned for Gen to come over.

As Gen approached the table, Millie said, "Sheriff Schultz has some exciting new information. They have arrested Tony Crow for Evie's disappearance. Some convenience store attendant saw a young woman in his truck at around six on Friday morning when he stopped for some snacks in Littlefork."

Gen's eyebrows went up. "Oh! Has he admitted to anything yet?"

"Well," the sheriff said, "I really can't reveal what we've found out."

"Okay," Gen replied, "I'm happy you're making progress in the case. It seems that you have left no proverbial stone unturned."

The sheriff's chest puffed up with pride as he agreed with Gen's evaluation of his crime-solving abilities.

Later the sheriff left the table. When he was out of earshot, Gen whispered to Millie, "I don't think Tony is guilty of anything. I think Evie planned all this."

"What makes you say that?" Millie asked. "Have you found proof?"

Gen relayed the information she'd gotten from the janitor.

"Sounds logical," Millie agreed after hearing Gen's story and theory. "Since you haven't found any of her old record books, she must have gotten rid of them for a reason. They probably contained information that would have proven she was messing around with those two senior boys. If she changed the records, the experts would be able to tell, so she destroyed them in the furnace."

Millie paused a moment to ponder. "I agree with your theory," she said. "Now let's talk about something else. How was your weekend?"

"Great. I didn't realize how much Fletch meant to me until he left. I've got to find a job closer to home. Life isn't very good without him. I guess one of the best feelings in the world is knowing that your presence and absence both mean something to someone."

Millie nodded and smiled in agreement.

"Marva is having supper late tonight, around six thirty, because she's helping clean the church. I have enough time to talk to my informant and see how the Evie case is coming," Gen said, getting up from the table.

"Have at it. Personally, I'm getting tired of the Evie case. The intrigue has faded."

Gen wandered over to the bar and slapped Charlie on the back. "How's your life going, Charlie?" she asked.

"Pretty good, pretty good," Charlie said with a big, toothless grin. "I have my good days and my bad days, dontcha know—but all in all, I'm doing good."

"Glad to hear it, Charlie." Gen smiled. "What can you tell me about Tony's arrest?"

"Not too much. The sheriff is keeping pretty closed- mouthed about it. But I have a friend who works at the county jail in Bemidji, and he told me that Tony denies any wrongdoing. Says he did give Evie a ride to Bemidji on Friday morning, after spending the night with her and sobering her up. Tony said that Evie told him she was spending Easter weekend with friends in Bemidji. Says he dropped her off at a gas station and left. However, they haven't found an attendant at the station that will verify Tony's statement. Kind of tough on Tony, dontcha know."

"Well, with all the people coming and going at those stations, maybe nobody noticed Evie," Gen replied. "She probably caught a ride with another trucker shortly after she arrived and left right away. She could have hitchhiked all the way to Seattle, where Joe was waiting to hide her."

"Could be." Charlie shrugged. "Anyway, don't worry your pretty little head about it. I'm beginning to think this is all a scam Evie planned to get out of some trouble she was in. That girl led a very secretive life that involved lots of men, you know. She could have been into lots of trouble or even blackmailing one of her married boyfriends. Maybe he paid her off to leave town."

"I never thought of that angle. Some married man could have been very willing to get rid of a girlfriend, who might even have been pregnant, for a few bucks," Gen speculated.

"You never know." Charlie took a sip of his beer.

"Right," Gen said, and then a light went on in her brain. "Didn't Tony usually deliver gas on Fridays?" she asked.

"Yah, but because it was Good Friday, he delivered on Thursday that week."

Gen nodded and motioned to Ed. "Bring Charlie another beer, and put it on my tab." Then she patted Charlie on the back. "It's been nice talking with you. See you around."

* * *

When Gen got home, Marva was busy making supper in the kitchen, so she sat down on the couch next to Benny, who was watching TV.

"How was your day, Benny?" she asked.

"Good. I worked on my pictures. Liz said she'd let me set some up in her store, so I've got to make lots and lots of them."

"That's great!" Gen paused a moment. "Can I ask you a question, Benny?"

"Okay," Benny said, totally focused on the TV set.

"I know you liked Evie, and she was good to you. Did you ever do any favors for Evie?"

Benny didn't answer for a few moments. He remained focused on the TV. Then he said, "Evie and I had secrets. She was my friend. I kept the secrets she told me. That's why she told me. I was her best friend in Little Beaver."

"What secrets did she tell you, Benny?' Gen asked softly, not wanting to sound like she was interrogating him.

Benny turned his focus from the TV to Gen. He looked at her like she was crazy. Then he answered, "Dontcha know a secret is a secret? You can't tell anyone, or it isn't a secret anymore."

Gen tried to be more diplomatic and explained, "Yes, I know a secret has to be kept, but sometimes you need to tell secrets to help people, you know, in case they are in trouble and could get hurt."

"No!" Benny said emphatically. He got up from the couch and stormed out of the room, slamming the door as he went.

CHAPTER 21

What we've got here is a failure to communicate.
—*Cool Hand Luke* (1967)

G en tossed and turned in bed, unable to sleep. Questions kept running through her mind. *Why is Benny so upset about secrets with Evie? Should I talk to Marva about this? Do I want to get those two in trouble because they've kept information from the law?*

By morning she was exhausted but had made up her mind to discuss the matter with Marva. *The truth is always the best policy for everyone,* she thought.

After breakfast, Benny rushed out to the shed to work on his pictures, and Oscar went to school to attend a before-school meeting with his Academic Pursuit Team. Gen stayed in the kitchen and helped Marva put the dishes into the dishwasher.

"Did you know that Benny and Evie had secrets?" she asked Marva.

Marva looked surprised. "What kind of secrets?"

"That's what I'd like to know," Gen said. "I'm surprised Evie would confide in Benny, but I suppose she needed someone to talk to and felt she could trust him."

"Well!" Marva said with a stern look on her face. "I'll have to get to the bottom of this. I don't want Benny in trouble with the law because of Evie!" Marva paused for a moment. "I'll wait until Oscar gets home from school this afternoon and tell him. He's really good with Benny, and Benny looks to Oscar for advice—like a father figure."

"That's a good idea." She paused a moment as a worried look crossed her face. "I don't want to get anyone into trouble, but if Benny can help solve this mystery, we might get to the bottom of things. The sooner this is all over, the better."

"I agree," Marva said. "Don't look so worried, sweetheart. None of this is your fault. You fell into a community mess here, and now you're trying to help us all get this straightened out— bless you."

* * *

When Oscar came home from school a little after five that afternoon, Marva told him about her morning conversation with Gen.

Oscar agreed to help. The two of them confronted Benny out in the shed, where he was busy making more frames for the pictures he had hanging on a bulletin board above his workbench.

"Benny, sweetheart," Marva began, "Gen told us that you and Evie had secrets."

Benny stopped working. Suddenly an angst-ridden look appeared on his face. "Gen shouldn't have told. That was supposed to be a secret!"

"I know, Benny," Marva said contritely. "Secrets are to be kept, but if keeping a secret can be harmful to people, then it's better if you tell."

"No!" Benny said. Then he went back to his work, ignoring Marva and Oscar.

Oscar went and stood beside Benny. "You know how much your mother loves you and has always done what's best for you? Well, she's concerned that you'll get into trouble with the law if you don't tell all you know about Evie."

"No!" Benny said again more assertively. He laid down his hammer and stared at his mother.

"I'm only concerned with your welfare and also with Evie's well-being," Marva said. "She could be hurt somewhere or even a prisoner. If we had more clues, maybe we could help her. It's always best if the truth comes out."

"No," Benny said with less enthusiasm.

"Your mother needs you, Benny," Oscar said, putting his hand on Benny's shoulder. "If they take you away, she'll be devastated. You know that, don't you?"

"Yes," Benny said, giving his mother a loving, sad look.

"Well then," Oscar said, "what do you think the right thing to do would be?"

Benny capitulated. "I buried Evie's diary for her, out in the backyard. Early Friday morning when she came home. She asked me to do that when I woke up and saw her coming down the stairs with a small duffel bag. She said it was a secret. I shouldn't tell. She'll be mad when she sees me."

"It's okay, Benny," Marva said, giving her son a hug. "It's for the best."

"Where did you bury it?" Oscar asked.

"Out in the backyard. In the soft dirt we'd dug up for the garden."

"Can you show us?" Oscar asked.

"Yah," Benny said with little enthusiasm. "Will they arrest me and put me in jail?"

"No, honey, I don't think so. You told the truth. You'll be okay. We'll see to that," Marva said with commitment.

"When you saw Evie leave that night, did you notice anyone outside waiting for her?" Oscar asked.

"No."

"Did you hear something like a truck running, down the street?" Oscar asked.

"I don't remember. She just walked out of the house and down the street. I went to bury the diary right away, before you and Mom woke up," Benny explained.

"Okay, honey," Marva said. "We'll have to tell Sheriff Schultz, and he'll have to dig it up so he will believe we weren't all hiding something from him. I think he'll do the right thing."

Marva got on the phone and called the sheriff. He arrived at the inn a short time later with Charlie.

"Good morning, Sheriff, Charlie," Marva greeted the two at the front door. "Oscar and Benny are in the backyard, waiting for you."

"Charlie came along to help dig," the sheriff informed her. "He can also be a witness to all this."

Marva and the sheriff went out into the backyard, where Oscar and Benny were waiting with shovels in hand. Charlie went to the sheriff's car to get a couple more shovels.

"Good," the sheriff said. "With four of us digging, this shouldn't take long."

The sheriff was right. It only took a few minutes, because Benny remembered exactly where he'd buried the diary. When they found the book, it was slightly soiled but still readable. The ground was still a little cold, and it hadn't rained, so the hardcover diary was intact.

The sheriff opened the diary and began reading. "This is very interesting," he said as he read the first few pages and then closed the book. "We'll take it down to my office and call the authorities. We'll need to put this diary into the evidence file." He looked at Oscar and Benny. "Thanks for helping. You did the right thing, Benny. This may help us locate Evie and question her. It should help the legal system straighten this whole mess out."

As the sheriff and Charlie drove away, Benny said, "Evie will be mad at me."

"It's going to be okay, sweetheart." Marva comforted her son as she put her arms around his waist and walked him to the back door. "It's going to be okay."

* * *

That night after supper, Gen called Fletch and told him everything that had happened since he left. "People saw Evie leave the bar on Thursday night around twelve. She was pretty drunk. She must have found her way to Tony's truck, which was parked near the convenience store. She spent the night with him and convinced him to take her as far as Bemidji in the early morning, to spend Easter with friends. She was probably going to take her diary along and get rid of it along the way—like she did her phone. But then, when Benny saw her leaving, she had to convince him to help keep her secret. So she made him part of her disappearance scam by making him an accomplice in hiding evidence and swearing him to secrecy. She didn't care about Benny; she just used him."

"I think you're right, babe," Fletch said. "What was in the diary?"

"The sheriff didn't say, but he looked excited when he started to read it; at least that's what Marva told me. The book probably records the visits she had with the two senior boys or maybe even had some evidence about the married men she'd gone with while teaching in Little Beaver."

"Do you think any married men were involved in her leaving?" Fletch asked.

"I don't know. If she was pregnant, she probably didn't know whose child it was. If some rich, old married man had been involved with her sexually, it was probably easier to get money from him than from the two high school boys who didn't have any money or property. It's starting to look like Evie wasn't as big of an airhead as we all thought. Her drinking too much was a big problem, but she seems to have been pretty manipulative too. She used lots of men—including Benny—to get what she wanted."

"Yeah," Fletch sighed. "Too bad she got Benny involved. He probably was convinced she liked him and he was special to her."

"According to her mother, Evie also suffered from depression. It looks like when she wasn't depressed, she was very active.

Maybe she was bipolar—you know, manic depressive. She certainly seems to have had ups and downs."

"Who knows?" Fletch said. "Well, now they'll have to find Evie, question her, and get the truth out of her. She probably needs help for her chemical use and her mental condition."

"Yeah." Gen sighed. "I just hope all the nice guys around Little Beaver won't get into trouble because of her." Gen was thinking about D.J., Tony, Benny, and a few more men she'd met and grown to like.

"Well, they should have known better than to get involved with a manic-depressive girl," Fletch said.

"It might not have been so easy to tell that she was bipolar. You know a lot of men, when it comes to women and sex, don't use common sense. They think with the wrong part of their body."

"I guess you're right about that." Then he changed the subject.

CHAPTER 22

Houston, we have a problem.
—*Apollo 13* (1995)

G en didn't notice Dawn standing next to her desk after the senior English class had left the room. She looked up with surprise, from the notes she was reading. "Dawn, I didn't see you there. You're so quiet. Did you want something?"

"Y-Y-Yes," the girl stuttered.

Gen stood up and put her hands on Dawn's shoulders. "Calm down. Now, tell me what's bothering you."

"I overheard D-D-Danny and Allen talking to another guy th-th-this m-m-morning at the c-c-convenience store b-b-before school. Th-Th-They said they were g-g-going to get you."

Gen studied Dawn's frightened face. "What do you think they meant by 'going to get me?'" she asked. "They're not even in school this morning."

"I don't know. B-B-But th-th-they were angry. They are m-m-mean guys. And they b-b-bully people all the t-t-time. I think th-th-they're going to sc-sca-scare you!"

"They've already tried that—to no avail," Gen assured Dawn.

"W-W-Well, then th-th-they might try something meaner, like h-h-hurting you. Are you safe at the Inn?"

"Oh, yes. I have Marva, Oscar, and Benny at the inn, and they would all help me if Danny and Allen came there to hurt me," Gen replied with assurance.

The warning buzzer sounded for the next class to start. The juniors were filing into the room for US history class.

"I've got to g-g-go," Dawn stammered and rushed off.

Well, Gen said to herself, *she certainly seemed frightened for me. Maybe I should mention this to someone else—maybe Millie.*

History class started. The assignment for the day was to discuss the causes and possible solutions of the Great Depression. The students joined in the discussion with enthusiasm. Many had heard their grandparents talk about the Great Depression, so they all had stories to tell.

The rest of the day went smoothly. At three thirty, Gen felt exhilarated. She was very happy that discussions and class participation had increased and the students were enjoying the lessons she had prepared.

When Millie stuck her head into the room, Gen was ready to go. "Be right there. I need to get my jacket."

The duo entered the café around five. The place was packed.

"What's going on here?" Gen asked with surprise.

"The whole town is buzzing about Evie's diary that they found yesterday. You must know about that. They found it buried in the backyard at the inn."

"Yes, I know about that," Gen said. "I just didn't know that news travels so fast around this town. There were only a few people there when the diary was dug up—Marva, Oscar, Benny, Schultz. I didn't think they'd tell anyone the secret."

Gen paused a moment, and a light bulb went on in her head. "Wait a minute. Marva told me Charlie was there to help dig and witness the discovery. That's how the whole town found out!"

"I think you're right," Millie said. "Everyone in school was talking about it. They all thought you had something to do with the discovery."

"What? All I did was get Marva to talk to Benny about the secrets he had with Evie. Marva and Oscar got Benny to confess about the diary."

"Well, you got the ball rolling. Someone had to get the people in this town to start talking about this mess. Once the floodgate was open, the water came rushing out. Everybody is confessing their involvement with Evie, now that they think this was all a scam and Evie isn't dead. I guess they were all afraid to say something before because they might get accused of having something to do with her disappearance. They all feel that the truth is now the best policy."

Gen shook her head. "Isn't it amazing what one rotten apple can do to spread stink throughout the whole barrel?"

"Yah." Millie sighed and took a sip of her beer.

"By the way," Gen said, "Dawn told me that she saw Danny and Allen at the convenience store this morning, and they threatened to harm me. I'm wondering what they're cooking up for me."

"Who knows? Probably some childish prank. Now that the diary is out, it won't do them any good to hurt you. The sheriff has the proof. Hurting you can only get them into more trouble."

"Yeah, I know, but do you think those two are smart enough to figure that out?"

"No. They might just want some revenge because they are probably going to flunk English and also get some kind of charges thrown at them for their involvement with Evie. They thought they had it made when they were blackmailing her for good grades. I think they're both eighteen years old, so they will be judged as adults, just like Evie. All three didn't have enough good sense to come in out of the rain."

"I guess I'll have to flunk them if they don't start coming to class and doing their work. Why doesn't Haugen get on their case for skipping my classes?"

"Haugen is a wimp! He won't take any action, for fear they'll get on his case!"

While the teachers were discussing the Evie case, D.J. wandered over to their table. "Evening ladies."

"Hi," both women answered with suspicious looks on their faces, wondering if he had anything to do with Evie's decision to leave town.

"What?" He looked hurt, wondering why he was getting the suspicious stares.

"Tell us what you're hiding," Millie said curtly. "Everyone else seems to be confessing."

"Nothing! My involvement with Evie was minimal, to say the least. I gave her a ride home from the bar several nights when she was too drunk to walk. I also invited her out to see my horses and dogs. She came one Saturday morning and spent the day there. She was pretty good company when she was sober."

"Did you sleep with her?" Millie asked bluntly.

"No. I'm not that desperate. It didn't take me long to figure out she was a few bricks short of a full load, besides the big alcohol problem she had. I don't need to get involved with anybody like that," D.J. said, glaring at Millie.

"You sure?" Millie asked in disbelief.

Gen nodded and smiled her approval. She knew from firsthand experience that D.J. was honorable.

"The rumor is that she might be pregnant, so if you did sleep with her, you had better be worried," Millie warned.

"Well, I didn't, so it's not my kid! There were plenty of guys around town that did, so they'll all have to prove their innocence, not me. A blood test when the baby is born should prove that—if there *is* a baby. Evie was quite a liar too."

"Okay." Millie gave up and changed the subject.

Marva had left a note for Gen at school that she was accompanying Benny and the sheriff to Bemidji in the afternoon to discuss what they all knew about the Evie case with some other West Coast law-enforcement officials who were working on the case. She said in the note that she wouldn't be home to make supper, so Gen decided to have a burger with Millie at the café.

After the burgers and beers, the teachers decided to play pinochle with D.J. and Charlie. The games lasted until around eleven, when they all decided it was time to go home.

"Does anyone need a lift?" D.J. offered, since he was the only one with a vehicle.

"No," all three answered in unison. It was a beautiful moon lit night and they all wanted to walk the few blocks home to get some fresh night air before bedtime.

Millie and Gen headed in one direction, and Charlie went the opposite direction. After a block, Millie and Gen parted. Gen walked slowly, enjoying the night air.

Suddenly Gen heard a faint crack. She stopped dead in her tracks. *What was that? Sounds like a branch breaking. Is there an animal prowling around the neighborhood?*

She took a deep breath and picked up her pace. *Don't panic!*

Some of the houses along the street had outside lights on. Gen couldn't see anyone or anything, so she slowed down, took another deep breath, and tried to relax. Her heart was pumping.

She heard another noise like something was moving stealthily from one bush to another bush that lined the sidewalk in places. She darted across the street, where there were fewer bushes, and crouched down behind a parked car along the side of the street in front of a dark house.

Gen waited, catching her breath. Then she heard a sound behind her. *Oh, God, there are two of them.* She bolted ahead to the next parked car. Her heart started to hammer from the exercise and fear.

Gen glanced around but couldn't see anything in the shadows. She started to panic as survival skills raced through her brain. She thought about her cell phone but then realized she hadn't brought it. She decided to run as fast as she could to the inn.

Gen tore down the sidewalk with her shadow gliding in front of her. She had been an athlete in high school and had enjoyed some success on the track team, but she was grossly out of practice.

She raced to the end of the block, where a large pickup was parked. She flattened herself against the pickup and rested. She heard someone run on both sides of the street, in the dark, keeping out of sight behind houses and bushes.

She could see the inn with the front light on one block ahead. She had to make a dash for it.

"Go, go, go!" she said loudly and sprinted full speed to the inn. The front door was still unlocked. She burst inside and locked the door. Then she ran to the back door and locked it.

"Marva, Oscar," she shouted. "Come help me!"

No one answered or came to her rescue. "Oh my God, they are both deaf!" she said, hugely upset.

Gen bolted up the stairs and knocked on Oscar's door. No answer.

She opened Oscar's door, shouting, "Oscar, Oscar, wake up!"

Oscar sat up in bed bewildered. "What's going on? Is the house on fire?"

"Someone chased me home from the café!" Gen answered, trying to catch her breath.

"What?" Oscar was still half asleep.

"Do you have a gun?" Gen asked.

"No! There are no guns in this house."

"Someone may try breaking into the house. We've got to hurry and get Marva and Benny up. I don't want anyone to get hurt." Gen was breathing heavily as the adrenaline pumped through her veins. She was having a conniption and not thinking rationally.

"Relax!" Oscar ordered. "Let's stay calm."

Gen took a deep breath. "Someone chased me home from the café," she said slowly and as calmly as possible. "I'm worried they might want to do me harm, and if they get into the house, they'll hurt you guys too."

"It's okay," Oscar said, getting out of bed, taking Gen in his arms, and stroking her back while trying to get her to relax. "I don't think they'll break into the house. Did you lock all the doors?"

"Yes."

"Good girl. I'll wake Marva up, then I'll go out and check on Benny. He's been sleeping out in the shed the past two nights. He's mad at Marva and me for making him tell his secret."

The two went down the stairs and woke up Marva. Then Oscar went out to check on Benny.

Marva and Gen sat in the living room and waited. About ten minutes later, Benny and Oscar came through the back door, still dressed in their pajamas.

"Everything seems to be quiet outside," Oscar said. "Benny and I snuck around the house and checked. Whoever it was must have gone home. They just wanted to scare you, Gen."

"Well, they did a good job of it." Gen started to weep as the anxiety drained out of her. "I'm sorry I put you all through this."

"Oh, honey." Marva came and sat next to Gen on the couch. "Don't cry. It's not your fault. This community owes you a lot— bringing this mystery to the surface. Now someone is trying to punish you by scaring you. How awful some people can be."

Marva put her arm around Gen and hugged her. Gen wept quietly, releasing all the tension that had built up during her flight.

Oscar called the sheriff to report the incident.

When Sheriff Schultz arrived, he assured them that he'd patrol the streets near the inn for a couple of hours, just to make sure the assailants had gone home.

The Jacobses and Oscar went back to bed. Gen lay in her bed, but she couldn't get to sleep, wondering what she'd done to deserve such animosity from someone in Little Beaver.

CHAPTER 23

There's no crying in baseball.
—*A League of Their Own* (1992)

Sheriff Schultz was reading the diary that started on August 25, 2012, when Evie had first arrived in Little Beaver and ended March 28, 2013 when she disappeared. He was enthralled by the juicy stories Evie told about some of Little Beaver's outstanding citizens. He highlighted the days and parts that were of special interest. The stories would suit him well in his reelection campaign. He'd make copies later of the pages he wanted to keep.

August 25, 2012: Arrived in Little Beaver about 4:00 pm. Checked into the Bumblebee Inn where I'll be staying …

August 27, 2012: Met the faculty. Got a tour of the school and record books. Had a teacher's in-service day. Learned about kids, faculty, supplies, expectations, etc. …

August 28, 2012: Started my classes. Wow! Kids are not very responsive. Lots of work to do. Went with Millie to the local café/bar. Met some cute single guys and a few interesting other men. Will explore later …

Most of September, the diary went on to tell about the troubles Evie was having in school with the students. She used words like *bored, impossible, disruptive, uncooperative,* and *discouraging* to describe her classes and students.

September 21, 2012: Called Joe to discuss my problems. He's the only person I can talk to …

October 6, 2012: Walked out to D.J.'s place. He invited me earlier. Interesting guy. He showed me his dogs, horses, cattle, and cabin. Also made some delicious deer stew. He has a way of watching me—like he's trying to figure me out. Creepy! I'm not sure there will ever be anything romantic between us. He's too intense. I like fun guys.

November 9, 2012: A trucker named Tony took me to his truck Thursday night after poker. I think he had sex with me—I'm not sure. I guess I was kind of drunk. Anyway, I was in his truck early Friday morning with a splitting headache. He had to move on and deliver fuel, so he told me I had to leave. He dropped me off at the inn. I needed to get ready for school. Bummer!

November 21, 2012: Mom and Stepdad came to get me for Thanksgiving vacation. I'm not looking forward to this. Stepfather is such a prick …

November 25, 2012: Glad to be back in Little Beaver. Stepfather was a hypocrite as usual, so self-righteous. I don't see how Mom can live with him—she's such a doormat. Too bad the bar is closed today. I could have used a drink. I'll have to get some booze to drink in my room during these emergencies. Ha! …

November 27, 2012: Poker night. I'm starting to catch on to this game. Hoffert gave me a ride home after poker—I think. Don't remember much. Must have gotten home early Wednesday morning. I don't remember sleeping much. The alarm went off way too early. Had a bad day in school …

November 28, 2012: Bad day in school. Most students didn't hand in their assignments. I needed a drink after school so I went to the bar with Millie. Tried not to drink too much, so I could make it to school the next morning. Called Joe to discuss my problems …

November 29, 2012: Senior boys are acting out in class. Making remarks about my drinking when they think I can't hear them. Danny and Allen are failing right now. They won't be so smart acting if I flunk them this first semester. Had a few drinks at the bar after school. Swenson offered me a ride home, then he got sexually assertive. I told him to buzz off. Every old goat in town seems to think I want to sleep with him …

November 30, 2012: Thank God for weekends. The kids in school are impossible. I guess I had too much to drink. Woke up around 3:00 p.m. in Hoffert's car. He said he'd meet me in Bemidji for the weekend if I could get a ride there. I've decided to go with Oscar, Marva, and Benny and tell them I'm spending the weekend with friends.

December 1, 2012: Spending the weekend with Hoffert in the Grand Hotel in Bemidji. What a self-righteous bastard he is. Talks like a big shot but cheats on his wife. I wonder what he does with his customers' money.

December 2, 2012: Hoffert dropped me off late Sunday night. Must have told his wife I needed a ride home and he felt sorry for me—stranded in Bemidji. She's got to be a total doormat.

December 3, 2012: Hate school. Can't wait until Christmas vacation. I don't think I'll come back. The way things are going, the school would be better off without a teacher than having me. I'd cry if I could—but that wouldn't help. Maybe I should talk to Haugen. He's such a self-righteous ass. He knows I've been having trouble with the kids I've sent to the office for discipline, but he never seems to give them much punishment. Things just aren't getting better. Called Joe, he sympathizes with me. Love that guy.

December 4, 2012: Talked to Haugen before class this morning. He suggested I be sterner with the kids and more professional. When I told him I was going to flunk about half the senior English class, he exploded. He said I couldn't do that. The parents would be in ragging on him. He's afraid to back me on anything I would like to do, except spend time after school each day tutoring the students that are failing. I guess I could do that. I'll start with Danny. He seems to like me, even if he isn't getting his work done.

December 5, 2012: Talked to Danny after school. He said he'd stay after school starting Thursday night. Maybe this is the start of something big …

December 6, 2012: Helped Danny after school. Things went well. I think he likes me. Spent the night in Tony's truck again—not too bad a guy. The only problem is that it's hard to get up for school on Friday when you have a hangover …

December 9, 2012: Lost weekend. Don't remember much. Caught a ride to Bemidji with the Jocobears. Spent the weekend with some guy from there—don't remember his name—maybe he didn't have one—ha!

December 11, 2012: Danny seems to be responding to the tutoring. A few other senior boys, the ones that Danny influences, seem to be handing in more assignments too. Things are looking up …

December 17, 2012: Bad day in school but a short week coming up. I think I can make it three more days, then I'll decide over Christmas vacation what to do …

December 18, 2012: Problems with classes and local men. Wish I were dead. Can't wait to get out of here. Took some booze along to school and hid it in my desk. I have to take a shot now and then between classes to get me through the day.

Christmas vacation entries were all the same. Lots of sleeping, lots of drinking, lots of relatives, and lots of arguments with her parents. Her mother was trying to convince her to go back on her depression medicine and quit drinking alcohol for a while. Her stepfather moped around the house, staring at her.

January 7, 2013: Back to school. Yuck! The only bright spot is Danny. I wish I could start my life over someplace else …

January 8, 2013: Danny's eighteenth birthday today. He invited me to his house after tutoring to celebrate his birthday with a piece of cake. Somehow alcohol got involved, and when I woke up it was early Wednesday morning. Danny hadn't told me about his mother being gone. Thank God he's eighteen …

January 11, 2013: First semester is over. Hurrah! I only had to flunk one senior English student, Allen Agindos. He's a friend of Danny's with a big attitude problem. Haugen was pleased. He called me into his office and suggested tutoring for Allen too. Now I have both boys after school Monday through Thursday …

January 15, 2013: After tutoring on Tuesday, Danny suggested we go to his house for a snack. It seems his mother works at a bar in Bemidji some nights and then spends the night with some guy. When I hesitated, Danny hinted that things might not go so well in school if I didn't sleep with him. I went, had a few drinks, and nothing mattered anymore. I know this is wrong, but my life is such a mess that I don't care.

January 22, 2013: Allen's eighteenth birthday. Danny suggested we celebrate at his house after tutoring. I didn't like the idea but Danny insisted. Too much to drink. I woke up early Wednesday morning in Danny's bed. Allen was there too. What happened?

January 25, 2013: Haugen called me into his office. He told me that he had asked the two boys I tutored to come see him and discuss their after-school sessions. They told him some stories about how good their tutoring lessons were going. He hinted that he knew what was going on. He also told me his wife was going to be with her sick mother for a couple weeks and that I was welcome to come and get some private help with my teaching methods on Saturday morning at his house. He said it would help me get better recommendations when I was looking for a new job next year. I hate that man!

January 26, 2013: Spent the morning with Haugen. Yuck! What a pig. I'd rather be with a mass murderer. I can't wait until school is over. Went off my depression medicine today. It doesn't help. Makes me more depressed. I wish I were dead …

The pattern in Evie's diary continued through most of February. Danny and Allen were blackmailing her into sleeping with them on Tuesday nights and giving them passing grades in English, she spent Friday nights in Tony's truck when he was in Little Beaver, and whenever Haugen's wife was gone, he would expect her to spend Saturday mornings with him. Some weekends were spent in Bemidji or Little Forks with a variety of men. Evie was drinking more and more, missing school at times for sickness, and growing more and more despondent as the days went on. She called Joe more and more to complain about her life.

February 25, 2013: I don't know if I can go on. I feel like killing myself. My life is a mess. The only time I feel normal is when I'm drinking …

February 27, 2013: Joe called last night. He suggested I come stay with him. I liked the idea, but I don't have any money to get to Seattle. Joe doesn't have any either …

March 6, 2013: Joe suggested a scheme. I can pretend I'm pregnant and threaten Haugen. He might give me some money, and I can get to Seattle, where Joe is. I'll talk to Haugen this Saturday. His wife is with her mother again.

March 16, 2013: Haugen was furious. He shouted at me for lying to him and not using birth-control pills like I said I did. After he calmed down, he said he could give me a thousand dollars from a personal account he had for fun stuff—that was it! He wanted me out of the school and out of his life. He made it sound like he was a victim. He said if I got sober and ever had another chance to teach he wouldn't interfere—big of him!!! I think I'll take his offer. Now I have to plan a way to sneak out of this town so nobody will know I'm missing for a few days. I need time to get to Seattle.

March 18, 2013: Easter might be a good time to go. I could catch a ride to Bemidji with Tony on Good Friday morning, since he delivers fuel on Thursday this week and there's no school on Friday. Nobody will know I'm gone until Tuesday morning when school starts again. I think I can get to Seattle in four days by bus or Amtrak, if I can get to Grand Forks to get on the train.

The next eleven entries were all about plans to leave. How to destroy all the records, how to lie to everyone about Easter plans, and how to keep from looking suspicious. Evie finally sounded upbeat in her diary as she planned her own disappearance.

Sheriff Schultz smiled as he finished the last page. It was almost a perfect crime, except she wrote everything down and then got caught by Benny when she was leaving. She didn't want him to tell on her, so she got Benny involved in her cover-up by enlisting him to destroy the written evidence. She knew Benny was in love with her and would do anything she wanted. She didn't count on Benny loving his mother more than he loved her.

CHAPTER 24

There's no place like home.
—*The Wizard of Oz* (1939)

"Have you heard what was in Evie's diary?" Millie whispered to Gen as she sat down next to her in the teachers' lounge on Friday morning.

"All I know is they found it in the backyard of the Bumblebee Inn and that Sheriff Schultz has it now," Gen replied.

"I got the scoop from Charlie that there are some really juicy paragraphs in it about some of our local citizens, including our very own Haugen." Millie smiled with glee.

"Really?" Gen perked up. "Tell all—please!"

"Well, it seems that Haugen was 'instructing' Evie on Saturday mornings at his home when his wife was with her sick mother."

"Oh?" Gen raised her eyebrows in surprise.

"Yes! And it also sounds like he knew about her disappearance. In fact, he gave her money to disappear!"

"Really!" Gen exclaimed. She realized at that moment that her fear of getting bad recommendations was over. *Nobody will read his recommendations after this gets out in public. He'll probably lose his job. I wonder what Superintendent Gray will have to say about all this.*

Millie took a sip of her coffee. "I guess they've released Tony. His story about giving Evie a ride to Bemidji on Friday morning and dropping her off at a gas station seems to be true. They now have the Seattle police looking for Evie and Joe. I'm sure they'll find her soon and bring her back. Maybe we'll find out the whole truth then—if Evie is capable of telling the truth."

"Yeah," Gen nodded in agreement while sighing in relief. *I guess that means there isn't a murderer on the loose in Little Beaver after all. I'll have to phone Fletch and tell him the good news. He'll be relieved.*

* * *

That evening after supper, Marva, Oscar, and Gen sat on the front porch to watch the sunset and enjoy the beautiful evening. There was a long period of silence as the three contemplated their own thoughts.

Gen spoke first. "I want you both to know how much I appreciate all the advice you've given me while I've been here. You're like a mother and father to me."

"Heavens to Murgatroyd! You don't have to thank us." Marva shook her head and smiled. "If I'd had a daughter, I'd have wanted her to be just like you," she said with affection.

Gen smiled back. "Thanks."

"That Evie sure caused a lot of trouble here in Little Beaver," Marva said and then added sadly, "Those poor boys will probably be in trouble for blackmailing and threatening her and also for being mean to you. They have confessed that they were the ones that chased you home that night. I think Benny will be okay. They gave him a little leeway because of his mental and physical challenges."

Oscar had been listening patiently and suddenly spoke up. "I wouldn't feel too sorry for those two boys," he said sternly. "I had a similar experience in the last place I taught, before I came here. I had a senior girl accuse me of sexual harassment because I failed her in algebra—twice. She wanted to graduate but didn't want to do the work, so her last alternative was to try and blackmail me into passing her by accusing me of something I didn't do.

Well, it didn't work, but by the time it was all over, I had lost my reputation in the community as a good teacher. Rather than stay and listen to all the gossip from people that didn't believe me, I chose to leave and start a new life someplace else."

He paused a moment and smiled at Marva. "This has worked out pretty good for me. I never would have met Marva if I'd stayed in that school. So you see, all this happening to Evie may get her the help she needs, and her life will be better because of it. Those boys did a terrible thing to that teacher, who was vulnerable and mentally unstable because of all the alcohol and depression. They need to be put in their place and learn to accept the consequences of their actions. They just can't grow up bullying people to get what they want."

Gen sat quietly and listened to Oscar tell his story. She had often wondered what a nice guy like Oscar, with outstanding teaching skills, was doing in Little Beaver; now she knew.

"How do you feel now about that girl who accused you of sexual harassment?" Gen asked.

"I feel sorry for her," Oscar said. "She obviously had some deep-seated emotional problems. I knew she was from a dysfunctional family, and God only knows what her life was like, but she needed to learn that you don't attack other people falsely to make your own life better. I hope she got some help. I don't know; I left the community and never looked back."

Gen sat quietly pondering what Oscar had said. She wondered if she could forgive Danny and Allen for what they'd done to her.

* * *

On Monday morning, Gen noticed a note on the teachers' lounge door: "Faculty meeting in the library at 8:45. Supt. Gray."

Gen grabbed a cup of coffee and headed for the library, where several faculty members were already seated and waiting for Superintendent Gray to show up.

"What's this all about?" Gen whispered to Nick, who was sipping coffee and eating a doughnut.

"I suppose it's about Haugen. As you can see, he's nowhere in sight," Nick replied casually.

As the faculty gathered, the speculation grew. Each teacher had a theory. None knew the exact content of the diary. Most of the teachers suspected the meeting concerned Haugen. They all knew about his sick mother-in-law and his wife's fragile health. Some assumed he was taking a leave of absence to take care of family problems.

Gray entered the library at exactly 8:45. "Good morning," he greeting the faculty. "Thanks for coming. I'll get right to the point, since our time is limited. Principal Haugen has resigned his position here, effective immediately, due to personal problems. I will finish out this year and try to do my job and his for the next three and a half weeks. I'll need a lot of help from all of you, because I will be in and out of the building. I've asked Oscar to take my place when I'm not here. Please bring your concerns to Oscar, and he'll help you. If he can't, he'll report to me, and I'll take care of things as soon as possible."

Gray paused and scanned the faces of the faculty. "Any questions?"

The faculty sat stunned. Nobody knew what to say.

Gray waited a few moments and then said, "You're all dismissed, except Mrs. Fletcher. Have a good day."

What did I do? Gen wondered as fear gripped her. She was having difficulty catching her breath.

When the rest of the faculty had exited the library, Gray turned to Gen. "Please follow me to the office, Mrs. Fletcher." He smiled. "There's someone to see you."

Gen meekly followed Gray, wondering who wanted to talk to her this early in the morning.

As she entered the office, she saw Graywolfe, Danny, and Allen seated next to the principal's desk.

Graywolfe broke the silence with a traditional Ojibwa greeting, "*Boozhoo*, Mrs. Fletcher. I hope we haven't inconvenienced you in any way."

Gen nodded and sat down, her eyes aimed away from the two boys.

"These gentlemen have come to talk to you," Gray said. "I'll sit here and listen." Then he sat down in the principal's chair and nodded to Graywolfe.

"Mrs. Fletcher," Graywolfe began, "you probably don't know this, but I am a mentor and father figure to these two young men whose fathers have left the family. Their mothers have contacted me to talk to you and represent their families in this matter of some concern."

Gen nodded her approval.

Graywolfe continued, "Danny and Allen want to apologize for all the trouble they have caused you by their inappropriate actions. They also want to talk to you about their English grades."

Gen nodded and looked at Danny and Allen for the first time.

Danny started, "I'm sorry I was such a bully and mean to you," he said meekly. "Graywolfe told us what we did was wrong. He said it wasn't courageous to bully teachers or girls. I'm sorry for all the trouble I've caused." He hung his head in shame.

"I'm sorry too," Allen chimed in. "Like Danny said, Graywolfe had a long talk with us about being grown men and respecting women." Allen looked down at the floor and quit talking.

Gen said nothing but watched the body language of both boys. She sensed from what she saw that they both looked remorseful and meant what they said.

Graywolfe again entered the conversation. "Danny and Allen have something else to ask you." He gave the two boys a piercing look.

Danny spoke up. "If you can forgive us, we'd like to ask you please to tutor us the rest of the school year in English. I can't speak for Allen, but I'll work my butt off and try to do everything you ask me to do. I promise not to cause any more trouble in class, and I'm really sorry we tried to scare you the night we chased you home from the bar."

"Me too," Allen echoed. "I'll be good and won't cause any more trouble. I'll even encourage the other kids to do their work."

Gen took a long look at both boys. "Encourage the other students but not bully them!" she said.

"Yes, ma'am," both boys answered enthusiastically.

Gen smiled. "Everyone deserves a second chance," she said. "We'll start after school today. You'll both stay for a couple hours and start making up all the assignments you haven't handed in or failed. You'll also do the assignments I give you from now on at night, at home. Do your mothers approve of this plan?"

"Yes," both boys answered in unison.

"Good. Then if we all work together, we'll be able to do this. You both have very good ability if you put your minds to this."

Both boys nodded obediently.

Graywolfe smiled. "Thank you, Mrs. Fletcher. I'll see to it that these young men keep their promise." Then he turned to the two students and stared at them with the look of a 250-pound professional football player getting ready to take someone out. "Now what do you two have to say to Mrs. Fletcher?" Graywolfe asked politely.

"Thank you, Mrs. Fletcher," both boys said meekly.

The trio got up and left the office.

Superintendent Gray smiled at Gen. "Well done, Mrs. Fletcher. You're dismissed."

* * *

"Line up, it's time to start," Gen shouted above the loud chatter in the entrance of the school gym.

The twelve seniors obeyed and took their places. They had practiced the day before and were ready for their grand entrance.

The school band began playing "Pomp and Circumstance." The seniors marched slowly, single file, into the gym, led by the high school faculty, Superintendent Gray, and Herman Jacobear.

After a brief invocation, all were seated, and the high school chorus sang several numbers, followed by a familiar march played by the band. Then valedictorian Dawn Kingfish and salutatorian Darrel Wanot gave short speeches and thanked everyone for helping them get a good education. Superintendent Gray said a few words and handed out academic-excellence awards. Finally the part of the ceremony the seniors had been waiting for all night was performed: Herman Jacobear handed out the diplomas, along with a handshake and congratulations.

The seniors marched out of the gym a lot faster than they had marched in. They stood in the entrance to receive congratulations from the faculty, parents, and guests. After shaking each senior's hand and wishing them the best in the future, Gen went to her room, where she needed to gather some materials to write the final tests that were to be given to the rest of her classes on Monday and Tuesday.

She heard a knock on her door. She opened the door and found Danny, Allen, and Dawn standing in the hallway, surrounded by the rest of the class. All the students were holding red roses.

Danny spoke for the group. "We'd like to thank you, Mrs. Fletcher, for being so patient with all of us." He handed Gen a red rose and gave her a hug. He was followed by Dawn, Allen, and the rest of the seniors. After the thank-yous and hugs, the seniors stood silently and waited for Gen to say something.

Tears welled up in Gen's eyes. She tried to speak but choked up instead. She took a few moments to compose herself and then said, "You kids have been quite a challenge, but I've learned just as much from you as you did from me. You all did a great job initiating me into the teaching profession."

Gen laughed nervously, and the students joined her with laughter and smiles.

After more hugs, the students took off for the senior party at the Café/Bar, sponsored by the community for all the graduates and their families and friends.

Gen promised she'd be down to the party later, after she took her things home.

* * *

School was officially over Wednesday morning, May 22, after the teachers turned in all their grades, records, and other school materials.

Gen said her good-byes to the faculty. She saved Millie until last, because she knew she'd break down and cry when she spoke to Millie. They had become good friends.

Millie was busy at her desk when Gen entered the room. "Hi. If you're busy, I'll come back later," Gen said.

"No, it's okay. I've always got time for you. Pull up a chair."

Gen pulled over a stool sitting in front of the room, sat on it, and began talking. "You've been such a good friend," she said and then choked up. With tears streaming down her cheeks, she continued. "What can I say? Without you, I'd probably have failed my first teaching job. How do you thank someone who's helped you through one of the most difficult times in her life?"

Millie smiled. "You don't. You just move on. You were a ray of sunshine in my life too. You're such a positive person. Always be that way—okay?"

"Okay." Gen sniffed. "I need to get going if I want to be home by tonight. I'll keep in touch."

"Sure," Millie said sadly, knowing full well that Gen would be too busy to keep in touch. "Good luck in finding a new teaching job next fall. I'm sure you'll be teaching in St. Cloud or nearby. That would be much better for you and Fletch."

"Thanks. I grew to love this town and all the people in it. I'll miss you all, but I guess nothing lasts forever."

"I guess not." Millie sighed. "You're young, with your whole life ahead of you. We'll all soon be a fond memory."

Gen smiled through her tears. She knew Millie was right. She would move on but never forget her six weeks at Little Beaver High School.

* * *

After finishing her packing and saying her tearful good-byes to Marva, Oscar, and Benny, Gen got into the Ford Fusion and headed out of town on the same potholed, root-filled gravel road she had come in on six weeks ago—now a much wiser young woman.

EPILOGUE

One year later

"What beautiful dogs!" Gen exclaimed, looking at the three black-and-white German shorthair pointers that were now a year old. "Which one is ours?"

"I thought Scout over there would be a good match for you two," D.J. answered, pointing to the biggest year-old dog.

Gen smiled and winked at Fletch. "Maybe we should get two, now that we've got a house and a big yard for them to run in."

"We've got space, but we can't afford two, now that we've got house payments to make!" Fletch replied. "Those dogs know how to eat!"

D.J. laughed. "I suppose you're going to the wedding this afternoon?" he asked.

"Yes," Gen replied. "Marva and Oscar are having their immediate family and a few friends in for the ceremony at the Bumblebee Inn, followed by a lunch—prepared by Marva. Fletch's mouth is watering already."

"I suppose you've heard that Benny has his own apartment now. His business is doing great. He's busy as a beaver and happy as a lark," Gen said.

"That sounds like Benny," D.J. replied. Then he continued, "Did you know that they found Evie living with Joe in a drug-infested house in Seattle?"

"Yes," Gen said. "Marva wrote me. I guess Evie lost her teaching credentials and was put into a treatment center for her chemical dependency and depression. I hope she gets the help she needs to straighten out her life. She's young and can start over."

There was a pause in the conversation, and then D.J. said, "Haugen took early retirement and he, his wife, and mother-in-law moved to Arizona. From what I hear about his wife and mother-in-law, living with them is going to be plenty of punishment for him the rest of his life."

There was another moment of silence.

"By the way," D.J. said, "Danny and Allen are working part time for me this summer, taking care of dogs and horses and making hay. Graywolfe is keeping the two busy until they start trade school this fall. Both boys want to learn auto-body work and then start their own business."

"Sounds good," Gen said with a smile. "That way they can vent their frustrations by beating out dents in cars and leave people alone."

D.J. nodded and smiled in agreement.

There was a moment of silence. Then Gen asked, "Have you heard anything about Dawn?"

"She did great at the university last year. She made the varsity track team and placed first in several events at the meets. She's on a full-ride athletic scholarship now."

"How about Bernie?" Gen asked. "I don't have the heart to ask Marva about him. I hope everything turned out okay."

"He's okay," D.J. said. "He quit his job and is working at a chain store in the Twin Cities. The sexual-harassment charges have been dropped, but he needs some time to get his life together."

"We'd better get going, hon." Fletch looked at Gen. "We brought a kennel to put the dog in."

"Good, let's load him. Here, Scout," D.J. called, and the year-old pointer came running, sat down beside his former owner, and waited for further commands.

"In," D.J. instructed the dog, pointing to the kennel.

Scout climbed into the kennel. Fletch closed the door, and the two men lifted the kennel and dog into the back of the pickup.

Fletch handed D.J. a check, shook hands, and said, "Thanks for this beautiful dog. I know I'm going to enjoy him tremendously."

D.J. nodded. "Sure." Then he looked at Gen, who was glowing with happiness and sporting a slightly rounded midsection. "When's the baby due?" he asked.

Gen blushed. "Sometime in October."

"Congratulations," D.J. said, glancing from Gen to Fletch.

"Thanks," the Fletchers said in unison.

"Well," Fletch said, taking his wife by the arm and helping her into the pickup, "we'd better not be late for Marva and Oscar's wedding." Then he walked to his side of the pickup and got in.

Gen shut the door and looked out her open window at D.J.

"I haven't written any poetry lately," he said softly. "I haven't had any inspiration."

"I'm sure you will, someday." Her eyes met his as Fletch started the pickup and drove away.

"What was all that about poetry?" Fletch asked.

"Nothing, sweetheart." Gen smiled at her husband. "Nothing at all."

Printed in the United States
By Bookmasters